2012

Moonwailer

PETER J MURRAY

SKYREFIELD

A Catalogue record for this book is available from the British Library.

ISBN-10: 0-9553415-6-6
ISBN-13: 978-0-9553415-6-4

Typeset in Garamond by Decent Typesetting Ltd,
Lime Kiln Business Centre, High Street, Wootton Bassett SN4 7HF

Printed in the UK by CPI Bookmarque, Croydon, CR0 4TD

The paper and board user in the paperback by Mokee Joe Promotions are
natural recyclable products made from wood grown in sustainable forests.

The manufacturing processes conform to the environmental regulations
of the country of origin.

Mokee Joe Promotions Ltd
21 School Street
Steeton
BD20 6NP

tel 01635 42567

www.peterjmurray.co.uk

To John Purcell, a wonderful friend,
missed more than words can express.

PROLOGUE

THE MOONWAILER

When darkness falls, the beast-boy roams
God-fearing folk stay safe within their homes
A creature born of folklore, legend, myth . . .
Superstitious banter . . . to entertain us with?
But deep within a craggy limestone place
The beast-boy lives with fur upon his face
Crouching, lurking, waiting, the bloodbath looms
He'll strike in shadow, 'neath the crescent moon
Fleet in foot, he bears down on his prey
Should it escape, the nightmares will persist until its dying day
And so my friend, stay clear the gaping Ghyll, the fairy dell
Lest you should meet the beast-boy . . . born of Heaven—
Delivered now . . . *from Hell!*

Joseph Cuthbert (Lead Miner) 1867

If out on't moor and on thar own
Ne'er go near yon standing stone!

Anon 1865

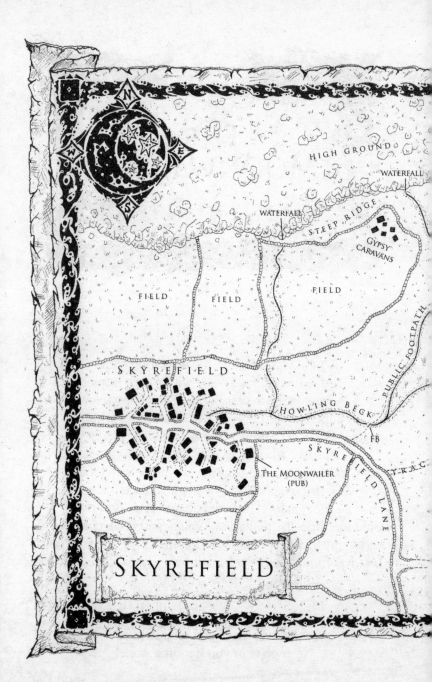

SKYREFIELD

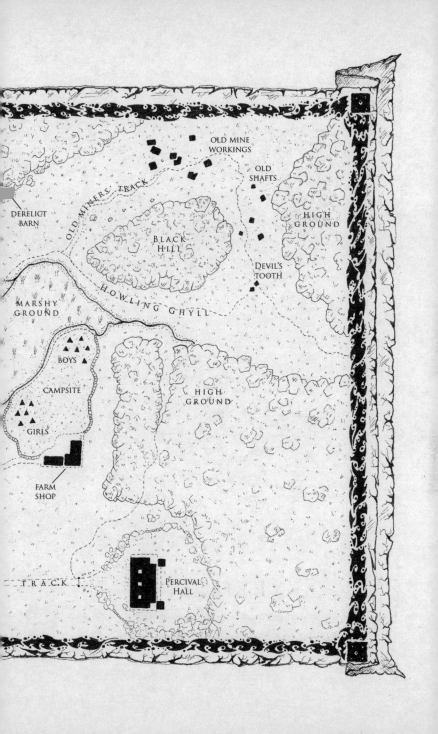

1
BEASTS

The night clouds drew back to reveal a full moon.

Billy Hardacre took a deep breath. His best friend, Calum Truelove, did the same.

They watched in awe as the man crouched beside a huge moorland boulder. He looked up at the silvery orb, and howled a blood-curdling cry that sent shivers down Billy's spine.

The man's face became clearer . . . piercing eyes bulging from their sockets . . . bushy eyebrows becoming lost in the thick hair sprouting across the entire face. His ears stretched until the ends were pointed and dog-like. Billy winced as the front of the man's skull cracked and groaned, the forehead extending over the eyes, creating the look of a horrific predator. Crouching down on all fours, the man-wolf creature looked up at the moon again.

Billy braced himself, ready for another heart-stopping howl . . .

'TURN THAT OFF!'

Calum jumped in his seat and spilled some of his popcorn on the floor. Becky walked over to the TV and turned it off.

Calum complained bitterly. 'What's *your* problem?'

Becky turned to face him – hands on hips. '*My* problem is that *I'm* responsible. Mum told me to keep an eye on you . . . you know . . . like a babysitter.'

'We don't *need* babysitting!' Calum snapped. 'Turn it on!'

'No chance! Sam's on her way, and as soon as she gets here *we're* going to watch a DVD. You two can clear off upstairs.' She picked up the TV guide and studied it. 'Anyway . . . what were you watching?'

'Parisian Werewolf . . . it's great. At least it *was* . . . until you came along!'

Billy nodded in agreement.

'It's an '18'!' Becky said firmly. 'Too old for you two babies.'

'You think you're *so* grown up,' Calum said with contempt, just as the doorbell rang. 'Come on, Billy. Let's leave the "girlies" to themselves. We'll go up to my room and play on the computer.'

'Brilliant!' Billy replied. He would never admit it to Calum, but inwardly, the horror film had been starting to get to him. He was more than happy to get on with the rest of their sleepover and go up to Calum's room.

*

It was almost eleven thirty when they finally got into

bed, Billy climbing onto the put-me-up by the side of Calum. Samantha Redgate was staying over too. She and Becky were across the landing in Becky's room. Calum's parents, Mr and Mrs Truelove, had just got home from their night out and were downstairs watching TV.

'I can't wait till Monday,' Calum said, lying back with his hands behind his head.

'Same here,' Billy answered. 'I've never been on a camping trip before.'

'You'll love it. There's something really cool about sleeping in a tent. It's a pity the girls are going – especially Kelsey Cartwright – she's such a dawk.'

Billy followed Calum's example and reclined with his hands behind his head, staring up at the ceiling. 'What do you think about the teachers that are going?'

'Well . . . Dude is OK. He's cool. But I'm not so sure about Dotty Dingle.'

Billy smiled. Miss Dingle's first name was Dorothy, but most of the Year 7s called her "Dotty" . . . never to her face of course. 'I know what you mean. She's a bit of a snob . . . and she really fancies herself.'

'*Just a bit,*' Calum mused. 'At least her tent will be over with the girls so she'll be well away from us.'

Billy yawned. 'Yeah . . . but we'll still be doing lots of stuff together. Have you been to the Yorkshire Dales before?'

'No. I've been camping before, with Mum and Dad, but not to the Dales. Should be cool . . . lots of caves and waterfalls and stuff. Dad's been there. He says it's a great place.'

Billy turned over and closed his eyes. 'I still can't believe I'm going. It'll be brilliant.'

Calum reached over and switched off the bedside light. 'Your mum's seriously good . . . giving you the money like that. Most mum's would have spent it on themselves.'

Billy smiled. Calum was right. She'd won some money at bingo and had immediately handed over most of it so he could go on the camping trip . . . *how generous was that?* He buried his face deep into his pillow and smiled to himself. He decided that tomorrow he would go out of his way to be helpful, especially in looking after Beth, his little sister. He'd make sure Mum had an easy day . . . let her put her feet up . . . then he could go away on Monday with a clear conscience.

He smiled again, his mind filled with thoughts of the Yorkshire Dales – tents, waterfalls and limestone scenery. He wasn't sure about 'limestone scenery' – Mr Duder, or Dude, as the pupils called him, said it was fascinating – but Billy had no idea what to expect . . . and yet . . . something inside seemed to tell him . . . whatever it was . . . it would prove to be extremely interesting!

*

Billy patted his stomach, stood up and began clearing the table.

'Thanks, Billy' his mum said, leaning back on the dining chair and taking out a cigarette. 'That was a good Sunday roast, though I say it myself.'

Billy nodded and continued clearing the table. He glanced towards the cigarette. 'Mum . . . do you have to do that?'

Beth banged her plastic cup on her highchair. 'No! No! No!' she yelled. 'See . . . Beth thinks the same. You know you shouldn't.'

Mrs Hardacre sighed and put the cigarette back in the packet. 'OK! I know when I'm outnumbered. I'll smoke it later . . . outside.'

Beth gurgled and made a noise that sounded very much like 'outside'. She was attempting more words now. Billy smiled and wiped her highchair with the dishcloth.

'Cuppa, Mum?'

'That'll be lovely, Billy. I'm going to miss you over the next few days. I hope the weather picks up, though. It's been so dark . . . more like winter.'

'Have you ever been to the Yorkshire Dales, Mum?'

With half-closed eyes, she watched as Billy filled the kettle and plugged it in. 'Yes . . . once . . . when I was a girl. It's a beautiful place. Lots of hills and rocks, streams and caves . . . gorgeous stone cottages. It's a magical place.'

She closed her eyes fully. She was obviously dreaming and thinking back to her youth. And then she suddenly frowned and opened them again.

The kettle boiled and switched itself off. Billy ignored it. His mum looked thoughtful. 'What's up, Mum?'

'I was just thinking . . . whenever you go on holiday . . .'

'. . . Something weird happens and I get into bother,' Billy finished for her.

'Exactly!'

He went back to making the tea and for the next few minutes no one spoke. Even Beth remained silent . . .

Billy passed his mum a mug of steaming tea across the table. 'I'm sure nothing will go wrong this time. Anyway, it's not really a holiday . . . we'll be doing some work on the trip. And don't forget, there'll be eleven of us from our year, as well as two teachers.'

Mrs Hardacre sipped her tea. 'Suppose so!' she said

quietly. 'But that makes thirteen altogether. You know what I think about *that* number!'

She put her mug down on the table and picked up the newspaper. Billy sat opposite and sipped his own tea. As she turned the pages, Billy looked across and saw a photograph of a boy with lots of stitches in his face. 'Mum . . . what's that about . . . on the back?'

She turned it over and looked at the article. 'Ummm . . . some boy got attacked by a pit bull terrier. It savaged him. Ugh . . . awful! He needed twenty-seven stitches in his face. The dog had to be put down.'

Billy felt a sudden chill in his stomach. His mum peered over the top of the newspaper. 'Are you OK?'

He took another sip of tea . . . felt the track of the warm liquid run down his throat and into his stomach. The chill disappeared. 'I'm fine,' he reassured her. 'That's horrible – being attacked by a dog like that.'

'You're right. Doesn't bear thinking about,' his mum agreed.

Billy drank the rest of his tea in silence.

His mum finished reading the paper. She folded it, put it to one side and smiled at him. 'OK, Billy . . . let's have a look at your tea leaves.'

'Aw . . . Mum . . . do we have to?'

Beth shouted 'Yes! Yes! Yes!' and Billy forced a smile. He walked over to the sink, poured most of his remaining tea down the plughole and swilled the dregs around the bottom of his cup.

'Good lad! Pass it here!'

He passed his mum the mug and stood back, awaiting her verdict. She stared into the bottom and frowned. 'There's something here, Billy. I can see a man.'

'I suppose it's me,' Billy sighed, 'grown up and about to get married to some nice girl!'

'Don't be clever!' his mum said, turning the cup in her hands. 'There's a man . . . tall, dark . . . he doesn't seem very friendly.' She looked up. 'I can't think of anyone like that. Can you?'

Billy thought for a minute. 'No . . . not really.'

He suddenly became interested. He watched as she stared again into the bottom of the mug. She looked up and frowned. 'There's definitely something strange here. We'd better be on the lookout.'

'What for?' Billy asked.

'*For a tall, dark, unfriendly man!*' she sighed, 'Maybe it's one of your teachers.'

Billy shook his head, 'I don't think so.'

She passed him the mug and he took it over to the sink. He carried on with the washing up and stared through the kitchen window, but saw nothing . . . he was deep in thought.

His mind went back to the Norfolk Broads . . . to the Bonebreaker. And then he thought about Aunt Emily's . . . and the Dawn Demons. Those holidays seemed unreal now, like bad dreams. Surely this trip would be 'nightmare-free' . . . just a normal school outing.

But then . . . perhaps his mother was right. Whenever Billy Hardacre went away . . . *weird things began to happen!*

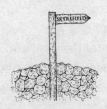

2
THE GREAT OUTDOORS

Monday finally arrived and Billy's school started its Activity Week.

The school minibus sped up the middle lane of the motorway. Eleven members of Billy's year group, who had chosen to spend three days in the Yorkshire Dales, chatted on excitedly.

'I hope there's loads of caves to explore,' Calum said loud enough for everyone to hear.

'So do I,' Matthew Moore joined in from the back of the bus. 'And maybe some steep cliffs to climb.'

Billy smiled to himself. Matty Moore was the best in Year 7 at sport. He always loved a challenge.

Kelsey Cartwright, however, was not impressed. She turned towards Matthew, 'And I suppose you think you'll be the best at everything!'

'Well . . . better than you . . . that's for sure!' Matthew sniped back.

'You think you're so cool,' Kelsey sighed.

Matthew ran his hands through his hair, 'Cooler than ice!' he teased.

The other boys laughed out loud, including Billy.

Miss Dingle turned round in the front passenger seat, 'Look . . . over there at the side of the motorway. You see those outcrops of white rocks? That's limestone. That's where we're heading . . . into limestone country.'

'I'm just about to pull off the motorway and then the landscape gets really interesting,' Mr Duder added.

The bus moved over to the slow lane and began to indicate. The Year 7s stopped chatting and gazed out of the windows. The weather was dull, the sky grey and heavy – the white limestone outcrops stood out against it.

Calum nudged Billy's shoulder, 'Look at that bird . . . above those rocks.'

'It's hovering like an eagle,' Billy said excitedly.

'It's a buzzard,' Oliver Wright-Humphries stated in a manner that suggested everyone should know.

Miss Dingle turned and smiled at him, 'Well done, Ollie! I didn't know you were an ornithologist.'

'I'm not, Miss. I'm just interested in birds of prey.'

Calum pulled a face and looked at Billy and the other boys. They all knew that 'Humph' was Dotty's favourite.

The minibus climbed the slip road to a small roundabout. It headed off left and entered an alien landscape. As the bus trundled along, Billy stared out of the window and became completely mesmerized.

Despite the lack of sunshine, the rolling hills looked magnificent – a patchwork of fields dotted with sheep and bordered with drystone walls. They passed ancient farms and quaint cottages spread along the road. They passed through villages full of pretty houses, adorned with hanging baskets spilling over with colour. Wild flowers sprouted everywhere, even from the cracks in the drystone walls.

His mother was right – *it was a magical place*.

The minibus weaved its way along the twisty winding lanes until the distant hills became more mountainous.

'We're nearly there,' Mr Duder said, turning another sharp corner.

Kelsey shuffled in her seat. 'Miss . . . I need to go somewhere!'

Miss Dingle turned and frowned. 'We're nearly there, Kelsey. Can you hang on?'

'No Miss,' Kelsey replied, her cheeks flushing slightly.

'It's OK,' Mr Duder sighed. 'I'll pull into this café.'

The bus pulled off the road and crunched over the gravel car park of *The Rambling Man Café*. 'Anybody else need to get off while we're here?' Miss Dingle asked, flicking back her shoulder-length jet-black hair.

'Me Miss!' Shannon Beardsley called out.

'And me,' Martine Hauxwell joined in.

'I'm feeling a bit sick. I think I need some fresh air,' Craig Green groaned.

'We may as well all get out,' Mr Duder said, switching off the engine. 'A bit of fresh air before the last leg . . .'

The Rambling Man Café was situated at the base of an impressive limestone cliff. The toilets were outside, at each end of the one-storey wooden building. Billy and Calum didn't need the loo . . . they stood in the gravel car park, hands in pockets, kicking at the loose stones.

'This is boring!' Calum sighed. 'Let's go over to those cliffs and have a closer look.'

Billy followed him, 'What's that . . . on the barbed wire fence?' he asked.

The fence ran along the base of the cliff and something furry was hanging from the top strand of barbed wire. The two friends walked over to it. 'Ughhh! It's a dead rabbit,' Calum uttered.

The other boys came out of the toilet and wandered over. Before long, everyone was standing around the impaled animal, suggesting various ways in which it could have got there.

'It might have jumped onto the fence while it was being chased,' Sam Davies suggested.

'I reckon it fell down the side of the cliff and landed on the wire,' David Jenson said.

Calum shook his head, 'No way. Rabbits don't just fall. And they're not stupid – they wouldn't jump onto it. I think somebody put it there?'

'What . . . when it was alive?' Sam said, pulling a face at the same time. 'It would have died in agony – *really* slowly.'

Oliver Wright-Humphries nudged his way to the front. He walked over to the carcass, leaned forward and examined it. 'It's my guess that somebody put it there . . . to act as a warning.'

'Maybe to keep people away,' Calum added.

Oliver nodded.

'Or to keep *something else* away,' David said in a spooky voice.

'Ghosts and ghoulies!' Sam said in an even spookier voice.

Mr Duder came out of the toilets. 'Come on, you lot. Let's have you back on the bus. We need to get to the campsite and set the tents up.'

The mention of tents caused a ripple of excitement and the dead rabbit was forgotten. But as they walked away, Billy found himself hanging back. Maybe it *had* been put there as a warning . . . *but by who . . . and why?*

He decided to go back and take another quick look. But Mr Duder was shouting from the driving seat of the bus, 'BILLY . . . HURRY UP! WE'RE WAITING!'

Billy ran over and climbed on board. As the bus pulled out of the car park, he took one last look back . . . the steep limestone cliff, the fence at the bottom and the furry corpse stuck on the wire. 'Do you think that rabbit was really put there as a warning?' he whispered to Calum.

Calum smiled, 'Maybe. Now stop worrying and chill out. This is one trip where we're going to enjoy ourselves and have some fun!'

Billy nodded and looked out of the window. Calum was right – it was time to give his imagination a rest and stop worrying – everything was fine!

But if everything really *was* OK . . . why did he have butterflies fluttering around in his stomach?

*

The minibus turned up a steep narrow hill. The engine roared as it worked hard to take the two teachers, eleven Year 7s and all their luggage up to the top of Scar Lane.

'Are we nearly there, sir?' Kelsey asked from the back.

'We're only a few minutes away,' Mr Duder replied encouragingly. 'Oh . . . now then . . . what have we here?'

As the bus passed over the brow of the hill, a policeman

appeared in the road wearing a bright yellow safety jacket. He waved and signalled them to stop. All eyes stared out of the bus as Mr Duder drew up and wound down the window. 'Hi there. What's the problem?'

The policeman looked at the two teachers and then at the passengers in the back. 'School outing, sir?'

'Yes. We're here on a camping trip.'

'And where are you staying, sir?'

Mr Duder pointed at the signpost across the road, *Skyrefield*.

The policeman stroked his chin, 'Straight on, sir. You'll be there in a few minutes.'

'So let's get there!' Kelsey muttered under her breath.

Miss Dingle swivelled her head and frowned.

'Are you in charge of this party, sir?' the policeman asked.

Mr Duder nodded. 'Along with my colleague here,' he turned towards Miss Dingle.

'Well, if you don't mind me giving you a bit of advice, keep these pupils close to you and don't let them go wandering. We've had a bit of trouble here during the last day or two.'

'What kind of trouble?' Miss Dingle asked over Mr Duder's shoulder.

All ears strained, awaiting the policeman's reply. 'Well . . . there's been a few dead sheep found in the fields roundabout. Most probably a stray dog. It's unlikely it'll bother you. In our experience, these animals usually strike during the night and lie low during the day . . . hiding . . . until we find them.'

'And then you shoot them!' a voice piped up from the back of the bus. Billy looked round. It was Sam.

The policeman ignored the comment and smiled at Mr Duder. 'Well, that's all, sir. If you do see any strays skulking around, be sure to get in touch with us . . . otherwise, I hope the weather brightens up and you have a good stay.'

Mr Duder revved the engine and pushed the gear lever forward. 'OK . . . thanks very much.'

'What do you reckon to that?' Billy whispered to Calum.

Calum shrugged his shoulders. 'Nothing really. It happens in the country all the time . . . dogs worrying sheep and all that stuff.'

'But that's the point – it's not just worrying sheep – *it's killing them.*'

Calum stared back at him. And then he laughed. 'Billy. Chill out! It's like that police guy said – it's just a stray dog – hungry for food.'

Billy nodded solemnly and looked out of the window. The brakes of the minibus screeched a little as it descended down the other side of the hill and entered into the village of Skyrefield. They stopped at some traffic lights by a quaint looking pub; Billy found himself admiring the stonework – greyish white stone mixed with flint. He looked up at the pub sign; it looked spooky. It showed a shadowy silhouette of a large dog-like creature running across the moors – the name 'THE MOON-WAILER' written above it.

'What's a "Moonwailer"?' Billy asked loudly enough for everyone to hear. Nobody spoke – the teachers were too preoccupied chatting about directions to the campsite. The Year 7s didn't seem to know.

'Oi . . . Humph . . . don't tell me that *you* don't know?' Calum teased.

Oliver turned round, 'Sorry . . . I didn't hear the question. I was reading.' He held up a book entitled 'Minerals and Ores of the Yorkshire Dales'.

Calum sighed. 'That pub sign . . .' he pointed out of the window. 'What does it mean?'

All the Year 7s were looking now. The creepy sign caused a ripple of interest. They waited to see if Humph knew the answer.

'The Moonwailer is a legendary boy-beast creature. A young werewolf. It's really scary. You wouldn't want to meet it!'

An eerie silence fell over the minibus. Billy swallowed hard. This time, even Calum looked serious . . . and Humph went back to reading his book!

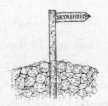

3
SETTLING IN

The girls had gone off with Miss Dingle to set up their tents over by the women's shower block. Mr Duder and the boys had finally decided who was sleeping where and were busy putting up their own tents.

Mr Duder was to sleep in his own one-man tent. Billy and Calum had offered to sleep in the two-man tent and the rest of the boys were happy to share the big, old-fashioned six-man tent.

Billy and Calum put up their tent fairly quickly and went to join the others. Mr Duder had sorted his own tent out and was trying to deal with the chaos surrounding the six-man tent. Everybody seemed to be arguing with everybody else – except Oliver Wright-Humphries – he was sat quietly on his own, reading as usual.

Billy and Calum couldn't help laughing. They were so

glad they'd chosen the up-to-date two-man tent.

'It's OK for some!' Sam called out, waving a tent pole and pointing it at Oliver. 'Why don't you come and help instead of sitting there reading?'

'Come on, Ollie,' Mr Duder shouted. 'Sam's right. This is no time to be reading books.'

Oliver stood up and looked indignant. 'Sorry, sir . . . I just got bored . . . what with everybody arguing and stamping around. In any case, I wasn't actually reading a book. I was looking at the instructions. It's an old tent . . . really complicated. I don't think you'll ever get it up.'

The teacher frowned and put his hands on his hips, 'You need to have a bit more confidence, Ollie,' he said smiling. 'It just needs a practical, common-sense approach. Would you mind shouting out the instructions?'

Ten minutes later, the teacher was studying the instructions himself and not getting anywhere. The boys started arguing again.

'Sir . . . I think I know what to do,' a voice sounded above the noisy chaos. All eyes turned to Billy.

'Be my guest, Billy. I can't make head nor tail of this.'

Billy took over.

First, he got the boys to put all the equipment on the ground. Then he went around arranging it in a certain way before ordering various boys to put various bits together. Within five minutes the poles were erected. He then rolled out the groundsheet, stood all the boys around it and had them peg it into the ground. He instructed them how to lift the canvas and ease it into place. Within another five minutes the inner tent was up, the guy ropes pegged in and the flysheet was rolled out next to it.

'OK . . . just ease the front and back holes of the flysheet onto the A-poles,' Billy ordered them.

'This is easy,' Harry Meanwood said.

'It is now that Billy's in charge,' Calum pointed out.

'OK,' Billy said confidently. 'There's just the flysheet guy ropes to peg out. Make sure they're tight, but not too tight.' He demonstrated with one of the ropes. The other boys followed his example.

The tent was up.

Mr Duder walked over and patted him on the shoulder. 'I'm impressed, Billy. There's more to you than meets the eye.'

'Billy, that was *well* good,' Craig Green beamed.

They all muttered their praises and went into the tent to sort out the sleeping arrangements. Mr Duder sighed and shrugged his shoulders as more arguments broke out from inside.

'Is it OK if we have a look around the campsite, sir?' Billy asked.

Mr Duder stroked his chin, 'Well there's still things to do. We've got to get the cooking gear out and set up the small storage tent for the food.'

'That's OK, sir,' Calum said. 'Billy can put up the food tent and I'll help him. He's ace at it!'

'Fine!' Mr Duder said. 'I'll get it out of the van. After that you can have a wander round – you've earned it.'

Ten minutes later, the food tent was up and Billy and Calum set off to explore.'

'Stick together and don't go off the campsite,' Mr Duder called after them. 'Is that clear?'

'Yes, sir,' Billy and Calum said together.

They walked away, heading towards the campsite entrance. 'Since how long have you been a tent expert?'

Calum asked.

'I'm not,' Billy said modestly. 'I only ever put up a tent once before. It was at Aunt Emily's. She had an old tent, and she let me put it up in her back garden.'

'Well you looked like an expert. I think Dude was gobsmacked!'

Billy laughed. 'Come on! That house by the entrance looks interesting. And over there . . . that looks like a shop! Let's take a look.'

The two boys walked up to a small wooden cabin in the courtyard of an attractive stone farmhouse. They walked inside. A girl stood behind the counter. She leaned on it, cradling her head in her hands. She smiled as they walked in. 'Hi! Are you two with the school party?'

'Yes,' Calum replied, looking eagerly around at the sweets arranged on the shelves.

'We're here for three days,' Billy said.

'You're lucky!' the girl frowned, 'I'm here all summer!'

Billy looked at her. She was slim, attractive . . . blonde hair scraped back into a ponytail. 'Why? Don't you like it here?' he asked.

'It's OK. It just gets boring . . . especially when it's quiet. Sometimes it's busy . . . sometimes it's dead.'

Calum picked up a tube of sweets and handed it to her. 'Well you'll be OK for the next few days. Things are never boring when Billy's around.'

The girl smiled at him and Billy felt his cheeks flush red. 'And why's that then?' she asked.

'Well . . . let's just say that spooky things and Billy go together.'

The girl took Calum's money and went over to the till. 'Oh . . . so it's "Billy the Ghostbuster" is it?' she laughed.

'Well you'll not be disappointed here. There's the Moon-wailer living up in the ghyll there.'

Billy thought back to what Humph had said in the minibus. He walked up to the counter. 'You mean the boy-beast creature!'

The girl gave Calum his change and leaned on the counter again. 'Amazing . . . you really are a ghostbuster aren't you?'

Billy was just about to ask a question when the door burst open.

It was Kelsey followed by the other two girls and Miss Dingle. 'Hi you two. Where are the others?' Kelsey asked cheerily.

'They're still unpacking,' Calum informed her.

The door opened again and Sam put his head round. 'No we're not! We're sorted. We've found something . . . come and have a look.'

The girl behind the counter smiled at Calum. 'Seems you're right – things are happening already. Maybe you and your friend should stay all summer!'

Sam shouted impatiently. '*Come on* . . . Billy, Calum! Follow me! You won't believe what we've found.'

'Wait for us!' Kelsey cried after them. 'We want to see!'

As they all rushed out of the door, Mr Duder walked into the shop and almost got knocked over. 'Just behave yourselves!' he called after them. 'We'll be along in a minute.'

Once outside Sam led them to the top end of the camp-site, just beyond where the boys' tents were pitched. The other Year 7 boys were gathered by a barbed wire fence.

'What is it?' Calum called out as they approached.

'Yeah . . . what's so interesting?' Kelsey asked.

'You'll soon see,' Sam replied, looking straight ahead.

Billy stopped and pulled Calum back..

'What's up?' Calum said.

'I've got bad vibes. My stomach's churning.'

Calum frowned. 'Billy . . . you're at it again! You're starting to freak me out.'

Sam shouted impatiently. 'COME ON YOU TWO! COME AND LOOK AT THIS!'

Billy took a deep breath and tried to appear more relaxed. 'Sorry! Let's go and see what all the fuss's about.'

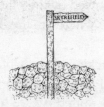

4
THE LIE OF
THE LAND

Billy gawped at the sight of the dead animal hanging on the wire.

Its fur, a striking autumnal gold, was splattered with blood, clotted and encrusted around its throat. The ears were still erect and the eyes striking in intensity. Even in death, the fox's face carried an expression of alertness . . . of fear . . . as if still trying to escape from its attacker.

'It's gross!' Matty Moore said, pulling a face.

'Ughhh . . . it's disgusting!' Kelsey moaned.

To Billy, the carcass presented a strange combination of beauty and horror.

'COME AWAY!'

The Year 7s looked around and stepped back as their two teachers marched towards them. 'I don't like you near barbed wire fences,' Mr Duder said firmly. 'In any case . . .

what's so interesting?'

'It's a dead fox, sir,' Craig Green informed him.

'And by the look of it, it's not been dead all that long,' Billy observed. 'Look at the eyes . . . still clear . . . like it's staring.'

The teachers walked up to the fence and took a closer look. 'It's such a shame,' Miss Dingle sighed. 'Foxes are beautiful animals. I wonder how it got there.'

'That's what we were wondering, Miss,' Kelsey said.

'It looks like something killed it and hung it there,' Craig suggested.

Calum took a step closer and peered at it, 'Like the rabbit we saw earlier,' he added. 'Do you reckon it's just coincidence . . . two dead animals . . . both hanging on wire fences?'

The other Year 7 boys muttered to each other.

'Can we cut its tail off and keep it?' Sam asked enthusiastically. 'It's supposed to bring you luck?'

'Ughhh . . . that's sick!' Kelsey groaned.

Miss Dingle folded her arms across her chest and turned to face him. 'It's a rabbit's foot that people use as a good luck charm. Not a fox's tail!'

The other Year 7s burst into laughter . . . apart from Billy! He looked thoughtful.

A noisy engine attracted everyone's attention and they turned round as a mud-splattered four-wheel drive rolled up beside them. A man got out dressed in an old t-shirt and cord trousers. His face was weathered and quite red. He marched up towards Mr Duder and reached out to shake his hand.

'Hello! I'm from the house over there. I'm the farmer who owns the campsite. The name's Jessop . . . David

Jessop.' The Year 7s watched as he shook hands with Mr Duder and Miss Dingle. He looked over to the fence and frowned, 'I see those damn travellers have been busy again,' he sighed. They all watched in silence as he walked up to the dead fox, lifted it off the fence and took it over to his jeep. He threw the carcass in the back and rubbed his hands together. 'Sorry about that! Are you all settled in?'

Billy sensed that the farmer didn't want to talk about the fox. He seemed keen to move on. But the boys were having none of it – their curiosity was aroused.

'Excuse me. Have you any idea who put that fox there?' Sam asked.

The farmer turned to face him. He looked serious. 'Like I said . . . travellers. They've got some funny ways.'

'What do you mean by "travellers"?' Calum asked.

'So many questions!' Miss Dingle said, looking a trifle embarrassed. 'I think it's time we were . . .'

'No . . . it's OK!' the farmer said smiling – though to Billy it looked more like a forced smile. 'Travellers are caravan people. They move around a lot and stay in some places longer than others. They've been coming here for years. They're camped over in the top field, this side of the village.'

'Why would they put a dead fox on the fence?' another of the Year 7s asked. It was David Jenson. He was usually too shy to ask questions, but his eyes were wide with curiosity.

'Like I said . . . travellers have some funny ways. They're a superstitious lot. They stick dead animals on fences to keep away evil spirits and such.'

'Do they really believe in all that stuff?' Kelsey asked.

The farmer nodded. 'Too true! That's why they always

camp by water . . . they claim it makes a barrier . . . to protect them. That's why they're up by the beck.'

'Is that because evil spirits can't swim?' Sam asked cheerily.

'More than likely,' the farmer laughed.

The other Year 7s joined in the laughter and the schoolteachers smiled.

'OK guys!' Mr Duder said. 'Let's head back to the tents. My stomach tells me it's time to eat. Boys . . . we'll take charge of the meal tonight . . . and then the girls tomorrow night. We'll take it in turns.'

The mention of food provoked a lot of discussion and the business with the fox seemed momentarily forgotten. Whilst the teachers continued chatting to the farmer and the pupils moved off towards the tents, Billy and Calum headed towards their own tent. Neither of them spoke until they were safely inside, well away from any prying ears.

'You've gone really quiet. What are you thinking about?'

Billy laid back on his sleeping bag. 'Did you see that farmer's face when he saw the dead fox?'

Calum knelt by Billy's side, fiddling with a big rubber torch. 'Can't say I noticed anything.'

'Well *I* did. He seemed a bit nervous.'

Calum put the torch down. He looked at Billy with a curious expression. 'So what are you saying?'

Billy stared up at the roof of the tent. A small spider had begun spinning a web between the roof pole and the canvas. 'Do you remember what Humph said back at that café . . . about the rabbit?'

Calum thought for a minute. 'Yes . . . he said it might have been put there as a warning.'

Billy pushed himself up onto his elbows and looked straight into Calum's eyes. 'Exactly. And that's why the fox might be there . . . *as a warning.*'

Calum sighed. 'Yes, but you heard what the farmer said.'

Billy nodded. 'Travellers . . . keeping out evil spirits and stuff!'

'Or maybe just to keep out that stray dog that the policeman told us about,' Calum suggested. 'The one that's been killing sheep. Why? What do you think?'

The spider on top of the roof pole finished its work. It moved out to the edge of its finely spun web and disappeared behind the pole. 'Well . . . animals mark out their territory, don't they?'

Calum nodded.

'So maybe the stray dog . . . or whatever it is . . . put that fox there.'

Calum frowned. 'I know where you're coming from! You think that the Moonwailer creature might have put it there?'

'I don't know what I think,' Billy sighed. 'I just feel uncomfortable . . . bad vibes.'

'BILLY . . . CALUM! STOP SKIVING AND COME AND HELP!' a voice rang out from somewhere outside the tent.

'Come on,' Calum said cheerfully. 'Let's go and help with the cooking. I'm starved!'

The thought of food cheered Billy up. But just before he moved off his sleeping bag, he took a last look up at the spider's web. A little fly had already become trapped at its centre and the spider was moving towards it . . . ready to kill its prey.

Billy felt a shiver run down his spine.

He leapt up from his sleeping bag and rushed out through the tent flaps . . . keen to join in with the others. The sound of distant voices – chatter and laughter – made him feel more comfortable. He wanted to be part of it.

'That smells good,' Billy remarked as he approached the cooking area.

'It is good!' Sam replied, stirring a pan of thick brown liquid.

'Hi, Billy!' Mr Duder called from beside the storage tent. 'Would you come over and get the bread? The soup's about ready.'

A few minutes later, Sam and Matthew were ladling out soup into dishes and Billy was offering around thick slices of brown or white bread to go with it. When everyone was settled, Billy took his own share and sat next to Calum.

'Wow . . . this soup tastes good,' Calum said in between slurping mouthfuls.

'Brilliant!' Billy agreed.

'Is it me or is it turning chilly?' Miss Dingle asked. 'It feels more like autumn than summer.'

'It's not you . . . it *is* chilly,' Mr Duder replied. 'And the light's starting to go already.'

Everyone shuffled closer to a large camping stove at the centre of the gathering. The remains of a large pan of soup simmered reassuringly, suggesting heat and warmth.

'It's like a campfire,' Kelsey said cheerily.

'Yeah . . . we should have a singsong,' Sam suggested.

'Not with your mouths full,' Miss Dingle ordered. 'Maybe later . . . after the pudding.'

'Brilliant!' Billy whispered. 'I wonder what it is.'

A short while later, Craig Green and Harry Meanwood were assisting Mr Duder in ladling out the thick creamy dessert. Billy could hardly believe his luck . . . rice pudding . . . his favourite.

'Don't we get a clean spoon?' Kelsey asked, looking across at Miss Dingle.

Mr Duder answered for her, 'If you want to go and wash your spoon then you're very welcome, young lady.'

Kelsey looked at the schoolmaster. 'Where's the sink?'

Mr Duder pointed over her shoulder. 'Well, there's a tap by the shower block, but otherwise the stream's that way, your ladyship.'

The other Year 7s burst out laughing and began licking their spoons clean.

Kelly made a face and licked her own spoon. It didn't stop her enjoying the dessert though. Billy noticed that despite being the last to receive her portion, she was the first to finish!

The light faded a little more.

'OK . . . before it gets any darker, I'd like the girls to help me with the washing up,' Miss Dingle stated. 'Tomorrow, *we'll* prepare the meal and the boys will do the washing up.'

'Fair enough,' Mr Duder said cheerily. 'And once you're finished, we'll have that singsong Sam suggested. I'll light a fire over in the barbecue area.'

Everyone agreed and the girls immediately set about collecting the dirty spoons and dishes. A couple of boys went with Mr Duder to help get the fire going. Billy and Calum decided to stretch their legs and wandered off towards the beck by the edge of the campsite.

As they approached the gurgling water, Billy looked up at the sky. The clouds were clearing away and the moon stood out in the distance. It was a crescent moon and it hung ominously over the outline of the brooding hills.

'Still thinking?' Calum asked him.

Billy nodded.

As they reached the edge of the swift-flowing beck, Calum stepped out onto a flat rock sticking out from the watery surface. Billy moved further upstream and did the same.

'This is cool!' Calum called to him. 'These rocks are like stepping stones.'

Billy said nothing. He was too busy staring down at his reflection in the water. The light had almost gone and his face looked pale and ghost-like . . . his eyes wide and staring . . . he decided he looked like a zombie.

As he continued to gaze into the watery mirror, a loud blood-curdling howl filled his ears. He jumped back, slipped off the wet, lichen-covered rock and fell backwards into the freezing-cold water . . .

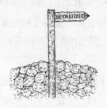

5
SPOOKY
STORIES

Mr Duder had lit a campfire and everyone sat around it sipping drinks, nibbling biscuits and chatting excitedly. Billy had been back to his tent to dry himself off. He sat in front of the dancing flames, staring fixedly into the bright glow, thinking about the horrific howl he'd heard earlier. Apart from Calum, no one had heard the splash as he'd fallen into the beck, but it seemed they had all heard the eerie howling sound.

'Are you OK, Billy?' Calum whispered from beside him.

'I think so,' he replied quietly.

'You weren't the only one who was scared,' Calum reassured him. 'That howl freaked everybody out . . . they're all talking about it.'

'Can we tell ghost stories, sir?' Sam called from the other side of the fire.

Billy watched as Mr Duder cast a hesitant glance in the direction of Miss Dingle.

Before the schoolmaster could reply, Kelsey spoke up, 'Yeah . . . go on, sir! Things are already getting spooky, what with dead foxes . . . and werewolves howling under the moon!'

Laughter broke out around the fire. Billy wondered how much of it was nervous laughter.

'Werewolves are no laughing matter,' Oliver said in a serious tone of voice. 'If you don't believe me . . . ask the Moonwailer!'

Everyone went quiet, anticipating that the knowledge-able Humph would enlighten them further. But he said nothing and just stared into the flames.

It was Mr Duder who broke the silence. 'There's a lot of local superstition in this area. I've been reading about it in my guidebook. But that's all it is . . . superstition.'

'Well, what about that howl?' Sam challenged the schoolmaster. 'We all heard it. That wasn't superstition . . . it was real!'

Mr Duder shrugged his shoulders, 'It was just a dog . . . maybe the one the police are looking for . . . nothing more.'

'Please, sir. Tell us about the local super . . . souperstic . . . whatever-you-call-it,' Kelsey pleaded.

Billy looked at Mr Duder's face flickering in the firelight. He was smiling slightly, but then the smile disappeared and he looked serious. 'OK . . . but it's a bit scary . . . don't say I didn't warn you.'

The atmosphere around the fire grew tense. Like everyone else, Billy was eager to hear what Dude had to say.

The schoolmaster began:

'There's lots of old mine workings around here. They used to mine lead . . . the area was rich in it. We'll be taking you to see one of the old mining sites tomorrow.'

Mr Duder paused and glanced at Miss Dingle before continuing. She looked just as engrossed as everyone else.

'Well . . . one of the mineworkers died tragically . . . in a mining accident. His wife struggled to bring up the two boys . . . they were twins. Eventually she married again.'

'So was she alright?' one of the girls called out. It was Martine Hauxwell. Billy wasn't surprised. Martine was a kind and gentle girl.

Mr Duder didn't seem to hear. He just carried on. 'Her new husband turned out to be totally different to her first. He was a cruel and callous man! He drank heavily and beat her . . .'

'That's evil!' Kelsey called out.

Mr Duder stared into the flames and continued, '. . . she died during their second year of marriage. After that, the twins were thrown outside and kept with the dogs.'

A gasp echoed around the fire. 'That's so gross!' someone blurted out. 'How could anyone do that?'

'What type of dogs were they, sir?' Craig asked excitedly.

'Never mind the dogs!' Shannon Beardsley said. 'What about the boys?'

The schoolmaster gazed around the sea of spellbound faces, 'One of the twins died. The other lived on amongst the dogs. He became beastlike and savage.'

Everyone went quiet – only the crackling of burning wood broke the silence.

Mr Duder craned his neck and looked up at the crescent

moon. 'A gang of miners set off one night across the moor. They were an angry mob, determined to bring the evil man to justice and rescue the surviving twin.'

'But the boy and the miner had disappeared,' Oliver interrupted.

'Correct, Ollie,' Mr Duder said, snapping out of his trance and nodding his head. 'You seem to know the story too.'

'I do, sir! And the dogs . . . they were pit bull terriers.'

'Correct again,' Mr Duder said. 'They were very popular in this area . . . and still are to some degree. They were bred to fight . . . sometimes to the death.'

Now it was Billy's turn to speak up, 'And the miner . . . and the boy . . . were they ever found?'

'Never!' Mr Duder replied. His eyes blazed in the fire-light as his story drew to a close. 'Legend has it that the boy still stalks these hills, searching for his stepfather . . . to avenge his brother's death.'

Billy swallowed hard.

'But he's not a boy any more!' Oliver stated confidently.

Mr Duder gazed up at the moon again. 'No! According to local legend, the boy became beastlike . . . more savage than the dogs he survived amongst. They say he turned into a young werewolf. The local people refer to him as the . . .'

'MOONWAILER!' some of the Year 7s blurted out.

The schoolmaster nodded.

Billy's heart turned to ice.

Miss Dingle stood up. 'I think that's quite enough, Mr Duder. I can almost hear the children's imaginations working overtime. They'll be having nightmares if we're not careful.'

Mr Duder stood up and rubbed his hands together. 'Quite right. It's time we turned in and got our beauty sleep. Some of us need it more than others . . . don't we Sam?' Everyone looked at Sam Davies as the schoolmaster gave him a friendly nudge with his shoulder.

Sam looked back at Mr. Duder and pulled a scary face. Everyone laughed . . . except Billy. He looked thoughtful and moved off with Calum towards their tent.

Calum yawned. 'I'm done in, Billy.'

'So am I,' Billy said. 'But I'm not sure I'll get much sleep. What if we hear that howl again?'

Calum stooped forward and unzipped the tent. 'You heard what Dude said. It's just a dog. Maybe a stray dog . . . I'm sure he's right.'

Billy followed Calum into the tent. 'Yeah . . . you agree with him now . . . but I saw your face when we were at the beck.'

Calum switched on his big rubber torch and hung it from the pole running across the roof of the tent. 'I'm surprised you saw anyone's face,' he laughed. 'You were too busy diving into the stream. What a plonker!'

The two of them changed into pyjamas and climbed into their sleeping bags. Mr Duder had said that they should go straight to sleep and meet by the shower block at seven the next morning. He'd also told them that if they needed the loo during the night, they should wake someone to go with them. He'd caused a snigger by warning them not to wee too close to the tents . . . if they couldn't make it to the toilets.

Billy and Calum snuggled down and chatted on about the day's events . . . about dead animals hanging from barbed wire . . . about the strange howling . . . about all sorts of things, including werewolves and pit bull terriers.

It was hardly surprising that Billy's mind swirled with a confusion of thoughts as he tried to get to sleep. The weather didn't help. As Calum snored beside him, the wind whipped up outside, whistling and moaning. The tent flaps rustled and twitched . . . as if by unseen hands.

Billy turned onto his front, pushed his face deep into his pillow . . . and finally managed to drop off to sleep.

*

He'd no idea what time it was when he awoke. All he knew was that he needed the loo and he needed it badly. Perhaps he should have resisted that second glass of squash at supper. The thought of the cold orange juice made him want to go even more!

'Calum! I need the loo!' He dug his elbow into Calum's side and tried to rouse him. But his friend just grunted and turned onto his side.

'Calum! Wake up!'

'Whassup?'

'I need the loo!'

Calum pushed himself up onto his elbows. 'Well . . . what do you want me to do?'

'You heard what Dude said. We're not to go out on our own.'

Calum reached up and detached his torch from the A-pole. He switched it on and looked at his watch still on his wrist. 'Crikey . . . it's only half-past two.' He shone the torch into Billy's face and dazzled him.

'Look . . .' Billy said, shielding his eyes. 'I'll just sneak round the back of the tent. You keep the torch on and shine it from the entrance . . . to give me a bit of light.'

'OK!' Calum said drowsily. 'Only get a move on . . . I want to get back to sleep.'

Billy slipped into his trainers and moved towards the tent flap. As he unzipped it, Calum sidled up beside him, pointing the torch to light his way.

'You should put a jumper on. It's probably freezing out there.'

Billy poked his head out into the cool night air. 'It's OK. I'll only be a minute.'

He crept out of the tent and crouched in the light from Calum's torch. The grass felt wet. It clung to his ankles and made him feel uncomfortable. He moved towards the back of the tent. Calum wriggled about in the tent entrance and followed Billy's progress, trying to light the way for him.

'Remember what Dude said . . . not too close to the tent!'

Billy smiled to himself and moved out of the torch beam into the darkness. As he stood there relieving himself, he looked over the wire fence towards the brooding hills silhouetted against the clear night sky. The crescent moon stood out vividly. The wind had died down and everything was completely still.

'Are you OK?' Calum called from the tent entrance.

'Yep . . . I'm finished!' Billy set off back towards the welcome light of Calum's torch, but for some reason turned once more and stared out over the dark fields beyond the barbed wire.

In the same instant, a blood-curdling howl rang out, echoing around the hills and washing over the campsite.

Billy froze. It was like someone had speared him with an icicle. He took a deep breath, bolted down the side of the tent, fell headlong over one of the guy ropes and scrambled through the door flaps back under the canvas.

6

QUICKSILVER

Billy tried to talk and clean his teeth at the same time, 'No one else . . . seemed . . . to hear it,' he said, making a spluttering gurgling sound.

Calum spluttered and gurgled back, 'Mmmm . . . nobody . . . mentioned . . . anything.'

'I couldn't get to sleep after that,' Billy said, drying his mouth on his towel.

Calum rinsed his toothbrush under the tap, 'I know. You kept me awake, tossing and turning. I'm still tired.'

'What are you two guys blabbering on about?' Sam asked from the next sink.

'We were just talking about last night,' Billy informed him. 'I woke up at half-past two in the morning – I needed the loo – and we both heard another one of those spooky howls. I don't suppose you heard it?'

Sam shook his head. 'No way! I slept straight through.'

'Lucky you!' Calum sighed. 'Anyway . . . changing the subject . . . do you think Dude will let us go into the village? There's a few things I need to get . . .'

'. . . Like sweets, for instance,' a grown-up voice sounded from behind.

'Maybe just a few sweets,' Calum grinned as he turned towards the schoolmaster.

Mr Duder grinned back at him. 'What's wrong with the camp shop?'

'They haven't got my favourites, sir.'

'Fizz Bangers!' Billy added.

Mr Duder smiled again. 'We've decided to walk everybody into Skyrefield before we head off to the mine workings. There's a few things *we* need as well . . . much more important than Fizz Bangers! And while we're in Skyrefield, we'll give everyone a chance to ring home, just to say that we've all arrived safe and sound.'

*

About an hour later, Billy walked down Skyrefield Lane with the rest of the school party heading towards the village. They walked in pairs on the right-hand side of the road facing the oncoming traffic, Mr Duder at the front and Miss Dingle taking up the rear.

'Look over there . . . we're following a stream,' Billy noted, 'it's right beside us.'

'Howling Beck,' Calum replied, 'I think it's the same stream you fell into last night.'

Billy pointed beyond the beck into a field occupied by a number of caravans, 'Hey! What do you make of those?'

Calum followed his gaze. 'Travellers! Remember what

the farmer said back on the campsite?'

Billy nodded his head.

As the two friends continued to stare into the field, a young boy appeared at the door of one of the caravans. He started waving.

Billy looked quickly away, 'Who's he waving at?'

'Us, I think,' Calum replied, tentatively waving back.

Billy looked again and took in the boy's appearance. He seemed shorter than Billy, maybe younger. He was wearing a hooded top with the hood pulled up – his face hidden in its shadow – that's if it *was* a boy!

'Do you think it's a boy or a girl?' he asked Calum.

'Can't be sure,' Calum answered. 'Anyway, whoever it is . . . they've got a dog. Look!'

The hooded figure patted a dog that had suddenly appeared by its side.

'Wow! That dog's really thin. Is it a greyhound?'

'Could be a whippet,' Calum answered. 'Greyhounds and whippets look the same.'

'But they're *not* the same.' Oliver came up behind them. 'That's a greyhound. A greyhound's bigger than a whippet . . . and it can run faster.'

'How fast?' Calum asked.

'I read somewhere that a greyhound can reach speeds up to forty miles per hour.'

'And what about whippets?' Billy joined in. 'How fast can they run?'

'About thirty five miles per hour . . . significantly slower than greyhounds.'

Billy and Calum smiled at each other. Was there anything Humph didn't know? They looked back into the field, but the hooded figure and the dog had disappeared.

The school party slowed to a halt outside a shop. Billy looked above the window and read the sign: *Skyrefield General Stores*.

'OK,' Mr Duder addressed the Year 7s from outside the shop doorway. 'You're allowed two pounds from your pocket money. You can collect the money from me and I'll keep a record in my book. If you want to ring home and let your parents know that you've arrived safe and sound, you can have another fifty pence. There's a phone box further down the road.'

They all looked in the direction of where the schoolmaster was pointing and saw an old-fashioned red phone box standing by the side of the pub they'd seen the day before – the pub with the spooky sign.

'Can I use my mobile, sir?' Shannon asked.

'Of course, if you've got one.'

'I haven't!' Oliver stated. 'Some doctors think that mobile phones could lead to long-term problems, such as brain damage.'

'Doooaaahhh! Yeaaaahhhh!' Shannon replied sarcastically.

'OK . . . let's get a move on. We haven't got all day,' Miss Dingle said firmly.

Ten minutes later Billy had bought his sweets and was taking his turn in the phone box. 'Hi, Mum! It's me . . . Billy. I've only put twenty pence in so I can't stay on for long. Just to say that we're here and everything's OK. The campsite's great! I'm sharing a tent with Calum. How are you, Mum? Are you OK?'

Billy paused and waited for the reply. At first there was a silence. Billy sensed the hesitation in her voice.

'I'm . . . I'm fine, Billy. You haven't met anyone a bit . . .

well . . . er . . . sort of strange, have you?'

'No Mum! Why? Who do you mean? You're not still thinking about the tea leaves?'

There was another short silence before his mum answered. 'I dozed off yesterday afternoon . . . on the settee . . . and I dreamt about this man. He was wearing a flat cap. He looked sort of old-fashioned . . . said his name was Eli . . . and that he was looking for you. He seemed like a nasty piece of work.'

'Mum . . . you're starting to sound weird. Anyway, I think my money's about to run out.'

'OK Billy! Sorry! It's just that he was so clear in my dream. And after what I saw in your tea leaves . . . I think you really need to watch out for yourself . . .'

A whining tone told Billy that his money had run out. He was glad. His mother had spooked him. He'd had enough bad vibes already. He didn't want any more.

As he stepped out of the phone box, Kelsey pushed past him on her way in. 'Are you OK?' she asked. 'You look like you've seen a ghost.'

'I'm fine,' he said.

Calum was waiting for him. Together they walked back to the store. As they approached they saw a small hooded figure looking into the shop window, a dog by its side.

'It's that little guy who was waving at us from the caravan,' Calum remarked.

The figure turned towards them. 'Hi!'

Billy stared at the round smiling face dotted with freckles, a fringe of bright ginger hair sticking out from the hood. 'Hi!' he answered.

'Hi!' Calum repeated. 'Are you camping in that field?'

The freckled face beamed back at them, 'No . . . we're

not camping. We live in one of the caravans. We moved here just after Christmas.'

'What's your name?' Billy asked.

'Elvis,' the boy replied.

Billy and Calum smiled at each other.

'My dad named me after Elvis Presley . . . he's a big fan,' the boy said, still beaming. 'You should see the inside of our caravan. There's loads of pictures of the King.'

'Which king?' Billy asked with a puzzled look on his face.

'He means Elvis Presley,' Calum said cheerily. 'All his fans call him the King.'

Elvis beamed even brighter. 'That's right. My dad says that Elvis was the king of rock and roll.'

The dog by Elvis's side whined and wagged its tail.

'What's he called?' Billy asked.

'Quicksilver.'

'Wow! That's a great name,' Calum retorted.

Elvis reached down and patted the dog's head. 'He used to be a racing dog. We found him abandoned . . . tied to a tree.'

A feeling of sadness welled up in Billy's stomach. 'Why would anyone abandon him?'

'Because some people are cruel,' a deeper voice sounded from behind.

Billy and Calum jumped round to see a tall figure looming over them. It was a man and the first thing that Billy noticed about him was his amazing hair – shiny black with a big quiff at the front. He was wearing a faded leather jacket, jeans with holes in both knees and a pair of stylish cowboy boots. 'Scum . . . that's what they are! They look after the dogs really well while they're racing and bringing in the money. But as soon as they're too old to race and past their sell-by-date, they dump 'em.'

Billy and Calum nodded solemnly and patted the dog's head. It wagged its tail and licked their hands.

'Come on, you two!' the tall man said looking down at Elvis and the dog, 'Let's 'ave you. We got business to sort.'

'OK, Dad!' Elvis replied. He looked up at Billy and Calum. 'Cross over the road and I'll show you why we call him Quicksilver.'

Billy nodded. Calum gave him a puzzled look. Mr Duder came out of the shop and began gathering up the school party.

'Sir! Can we cross over?' Billy asked. 'That boy . . .' he pointed in the direction of Elvis, '. . . he wants to show us something.'

'We're heading over there anyway.' Mr Duder said. 'OK, you guys! When I give the signal, everyone cross together!'

Billy watched Elvis and his dad make their way through a gap in a drystone wall on the other side of the road. They crossed a small bridge spanning the beck and Elvis grabbed hold of the dog's collar and waited.

A few minutes later, the school party had crossed over and were lined up against the wall.

'WATCH THIS!' Elvis shouted to them.

They all watched as Elvis let go of the dog's collar.

In a split second the dog set off at great speed, sprinting towards the top edge of a large field. Billy gasped as the dog accelerated rapidly with every step. Within seconds, it had reached the top left-hand corner and showed no signs of slowing down.

'Wow!' Calum sighed. 'No wonder they call him "Quicksilver"!'

A buzz of excitement rippled through the school party as the dog continued its journey.

'That dog is so cool!' Matthew Moore shouted.

Billy smiled to himself – not even Matty, the best runner in the school, would be any match for this animal.

The dog was on the return leg of its circuit now. Sleek and graceful it shot down the right-hand side of the field, turned the bottom corner and sprinted back towards them.

'GOOD BOY!' Elvis shouted through cupped hands.

The dog responded by accelerating to its maximum speed. It bounded back and ground to a halt, panting and wagging its tail excitedly, as Elvis patted it affectionately.

Billy, Calum and the rest of the party applauded and shouted compliments. Elvis looked across at them and gave them a 'thumbs up' sign.

'OK, guys!' Mr Duder called to everyone. 'Now that the entertainment's over, it's time to move on. Walking in pairs please. I'll take the front. Miss Dingle . . . would you mind taking up the rear?'

Billy and Calum stayed back with Miss Dingle. Billy took a last look over his shoulder and waved to Elvis, who immediately waved back . . . and Billy felt a tinge of nervousness. *He sensed that he was going to meet up with Elvis and his dog again . . . under different circumstances!*

'Move on a bit, Billy. Keep up with Calum,' Miss Dingle said cheerfully. 'We've a long walk ahead of us.'

'Sorry, Miss!' Billy apologised. 'I was just dreaming a bit.'

Calum turned and stared at him. Billy guessed the reason why. Whenever dreams and Billy Hardacre were mentioned in the same breath, you could guarantee that trouble was waiting around the corner!

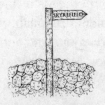

7
WARNINGS

As the school party left the village and walked back in the direction of the campsite, the wind sprung up. Small white clouds scurried through the bright blue sky. The sun peeped in and out, the light changing constantly as it washed over the dramatic limestone scenery.

Ten minutes later, the schoolmaster paused at the head of the procession.

'As you can see . . .' Mr Duder called back over his shoulder, '. . . the campsite is over there on our right. We're heading on past it in a northerly direction towards the old mine workings.'

Billy looked over the heads of his school-friends and saw Mr Duder unfolding his map. 'We'll take five,' the schoolmaster said in a voice loud enough for everyone to hear.

While he studied his map, some of the group sat down amongst the clumps of course grass; others sat on limestone rocks straggling the footpath.

'How much further, sir?' Kelsey sighed.

'Aaawww . . . are we tired?' Sam teased.

'It's at least another ten miles, isn't it sir?' Matthew asked with a grin.

'Yeah . . . right!' Kelsey retorted. 'They're lying, aren't they sir?'

Oliver, who was leaning over Mr Duder's shoulder and peering at the map, straightened up and turned towards them. 'By my estimation, the mining site is about one mile further on. It'll take us about twenty minutes . . . if we push on at a good pace.'

Mr Duder stood up, put his hands on his hips and smiled. 'As usual, Ollie's got it about right. We'll move on and have a rest and something to drink as soon as we get there.'

'But sir . . . we've only just got *here*,' Kelsey complained, 'Can't we have a rest now?'

'OK . . . take another five!' Mr Duder sighed.

Calum whispered in Billy's ear. 'Trust her to slow us down.'

Billy nodded and scanned his surroundings.

The campsite stood out in the distance, most of the tents brightly coloured and gleaming in the sunshine. To their left, just across from where they were sitting, a huge hill loomed up. It was strewn with white rocks . . . lumps of limestone, as Mr Duder kept pointing out. The top of the hill was edged with bigger more dramatic outcrops of white stone . . . "crags" . . . Humph had called them. Billy stared up at them . . . they looked sheer and dangerous.

Several trees, gnarled and twisted, sprouted from the top of the crags, their branches reaching out to the skyline like grasping fingers.

'What are you staring at?' Calum asked quietly.

Billy didn't answer. He was too intent on taking in the scene.

From where they were sitting, the footpath carried on towards a distant stone building and disappeared behind it. The stream, which they had followed up from the village, bubbled and gurgled alongside the path, edged with dense patches of ferns.

Suddenly Billy felt compelled to look back to the skyline. The sun had popped out from behind a cloud and it forced him to shield his eyes. He thought he detected a movement . . . behind one of the twisted trees . . . a fleeting glimpse . . . a black shape . . . a dog perhaps?

Calum nudged his arm and offered him a swig from his canned drink.

'What're you looking at, Billy?'

'Billy turned and looked Calum squarely in the eye. *I don't know . . . but I'm sure I saw something. I think we're being watched!!*'

*

Mr Duder allowed them ten minutes rest before insisting that they continue on their way to the mining site.

'Awww . . . sir! We've just got comfortable. Can we have a bit longer?' Kelsey pleaded.

'Here we go again!' Sam jeered, his pack already on his back and ready to go.

Kelsey ignored him. Billy and Calum and a few of the other boys sighed.

'OK, GUYS . . . FOLLOW ME!' Mr Duder called as he headed away up the footpath. Billy and Calum dropped back again, just a little way in front of the girls.

Billy thought back to the movement he'd seen earlier. A shiver rattled down his spine. The feeling that they were being watched was stronger than ever.

Calum seemed to read his mind. 'Are you still thinking about that thing you thought you saw? It was probably some kind of animal . . . maybe a goat or something.'

'Maybe,' Billy said quietly. 'Do they have goats out here?'

'Not sure! Could've been a sheep. There's loads of sheep.'

Billy scratched his ear. 'Definitely not a sheep . . . I saw it move . . . too fast!'

'You boys move on ahead,' Miss Dingle called out from behind. 'Kelsey and Shannon are just going to duck behind this building! We'll catch up!'

The building turned out to be a ruined barn . . . several holes in the roof . . . gaps in the walls . . . lots of heavy stones lying scattered on the ground. As Billy and the other boys filed past, a flock of birds shot out from one of the holes in the roof. They curled in an upwards spiral towards the sky.

'Something disturbed those birds,' Billy said quietly.

'The girls did!' Calum chuckled. 'Calm down, Billy! Don't get carried away.'

Mr Duder stopped and raised his hand. 'OK! Just hang on for a minute. We'll wait for Miss Dingle and the girls to catch up.'

A few seconds later Billy and the rest of the party almost jumped out of their skins as a piercing scream reached their ears.

'Blimey! What's happened?' Craig Green asked in a shocked voice.

They all spun round as Miss Dingle appeared from behind the barn, Kelsey and Shannon clinging to her arm. Both girls were pale and shaking.

'What's wrong?' Mr Duder said, walking back towards them. He looked hard at Miss Dingle. 'Why did they scream?'

'That's just it, sir,' Kelsey replied, her voice trembling. 'It wasn't us that screamed. It was something else . . .' she pointed towards the stone barn. '. . . In there . . . *it was something in there!*'

Without a word Mr Duder set off round the back of the barn. Billy, Calum and a few of the other boys followed.

The doors of the barn were half-rotten and hanging off rusted hinges. A small dark space between them formed an entry hole and Mr Duder crouched low and peered through.

The other boys crept up behind him.

'Can you see anything, sir?' David Jenson whispered.

'Keep back,' Mr Duder said, still peering through the hole. 'There is something in there. I can hear it moving about.'

Billy felt the hairs on the back of his neck stand on end. He whispered nervously to Calum. 'I told you we were being watched. I don't like it!'

Miss Dingle and the girls came up behind them.

Now, the entire school party were standing around in a half circle at the back of the crouching schoolmaster. 'Can you see anything?' Miss Dingle asked nervously.

Mr Duder had no chance to reply. A second piercing

scream rang through the dilapidated barn causing the startled schoolmaster to jump backwards. The rest of the party backed away.

As Mr Duder stood up and dusted himself down, Oliver stepped forward and said in a very loud and confident voice, 'DON'T WORRY . . . I KNOW EXACTLY WHAT IT IS . . . IT'S WILD . . . AND UGLY . . . AND . . .'

Before he had chance to finish, the thing in the barn screamed again. But this time it leapt out from the dark entrance hole and charged straight at the group of spectators . . .

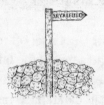

8
HIDEY HOLES

'**S**AM DAVIES!' Kelsey yelled in relief.

'SAM DAVIES!' Mr Duder and Miss Dingle exclaimed together.

'Humph got it right again' Matthew laughed, 'Definitely wild and *definitely* ugly . . . *ughhh!*'

Billy laughed. Calum laughed. And then everyone began to laugh. Even Mr Duder and Miss Dingle saw the funny side and joined in.

'OK! That's enough! Follow on!' Mr Duder ordered.

The party reassembled into a line and moved off, this time, Billy and Calum up at the front, directly behind Mr Duder. As they walked on, they chatted about recent events and the possibilities of what lay ahead.

'I still think we're being watched,' Billy said quietly.

'Why?' Calum asked.

'I can just feel it.'

Calum looked ahead anxiously. 'I suppose it's your sixth sense. We'd better keep an eye out.'

Billy nodded. It wasn't the first time he'd had these feelings and both he and Calum knew only too well the strange events that had followed.

After walking on for ten more minutes, Billy saw that the footpath ran alongside the edge of a large rectangular hollow – about the size of three or four football fields.

'This used to be a reservoir,' Mr Duder called over his shoulder. 'It provided water for the mining site, which is just a bit further on. If you look carefully you can see the bricks of the old dam wall over there.'

Billy looked to his right where Mr Duder was pointing and saw several layers of limestone blocks half-hidden beneath a tangle of grass and purple-headed thistles.

As they trudged on, the footpath climbed up and skirted the side of a steep hill on their left. To their right, the beck gurgled far down below, following its course across the bottom of the old reservoir.

'It seems like we're heading into the middle of nowhere,' Calum said quietly.

Billy didn't answer . . . he was too busy staring around.

They reached the far end of the old reservoir and the path dropped down again to rejoin the beck. Another large hill loomed in front.

'That's Black Hill,' Mr Duder informed them. 'You'll see that the path forks left and right around the base of the hill. 'We're going to the left . . . it's the track that the miners used.'

'Where does the right fork go to, sir?' Matthew asked.

'Umm . . . well . . .' the schoolmaster looked hesitant. 'I'll tell you later. We might come back that way. OK! Follow on . . . and no lagging behind. Not much further!'

They followed the schoolmaster along the old mining track to the left of Black Hill. At first the broad footpath climbed steeply and it was hard work. But then the path levelled out. As they trudged on, Billy noted that the springy grass beneath their feet began to disappear . . . replaced by crunchy gravel.

'Almost there!' Mr Duder called over his shoulder. 'See how the ground has levelled and widened out? The mining site is just through that gate up ahead.'

A little further on a crumbling drystone wall marked the boundary of the site and a broken-down gate carried a sign:

CAUTION: MINE WORKINGS
STAY CLEAR OF SHAFTS

Whilst Mr Duder waited for the others to catch up, Billy and Calum leaned on the gate and looked over it.

'Wow! What do you make of that?' Calum asked.

Billy looked out across the wide clearing. Over to the left a crumbling stone building without a roof stood beside what looked like some old railway lines. Behind the building, up in the hillside there was an ominous black opening with some sort of twisted metal grill straggling the entrance.

'Wow! A cave! Brilliant!' Billy said, feeling half nervous and half excited.

'It's one of the old mines,' Mr Duder said, leaning on the gate beside them. 'If you look carefully, you'll see a good few more.'

'There's one!' Calum said, pointing up the hillside on

the right.

Billy looked to where Calum was pointing and saw another dark entrance.

When everyone had caught up, Miss Dingle joined Mr Duder and the two teachers exchanged a few words. It was Miss Dingle who turned and addressed the Year 7s:

'Now listen to me, everyone. It's not hard to imagine the dangers surrounding these mine workings. After we've gone through the gate, we'll be surrounded by old mine-shafts, derelict buildings, sharp metal, heavy stones and goodness knows what else.'

'Steep limestone cliffs, miss,' Sam added. 'Easy to climb up and then fall down again.'

'Exactly!' Miss Dingle continued. 'This site is full of hazards, but Mr Duder and I are very keen to make this a "hands on" exercise. So please be extremely careful at all times.'

Billy wasn't sure what Miss Dingle meant by a 'hands on' exercise, but he was definitely in agreement that the old mining site looked dangerous.

'OK!' Mr Duder shouted. 'We're going onto the site. Follow me!'

He opened the half-rotten five-bar gate and moved through, the rest of the party following close behind. Miss Dingle closed the gate after them.

'We'll head over to that stone building and find some-where to sit,' Mr Duder said enthusiastically.

A buzz of excitement rippled through the school party as they walked across the dusty clearing. The landscape reminded Billy of a western film set. He half expected to see a posse of cowboys, guns blazing and riding towards them.

'OK!' Mr Duder said. 'This will do nicely. Find somewhere to sit and I'll tell you what I want you to do.'

'Are we going into any of the mines, sir?'

'Be patient, Matthew,' Miss Dingle replied. 'Wait and see what Mr Duder has to say.'

At first the schoolmaster said nothing. He was too busy opening his rucksack and removing a bundle of blue plastic clipboards. He handed half of them to Martine and half to David.

'Would you give these out, please? There should be enough for one each.'

A few moments later everyone was studying their clipboards as Mr Duder went through the questions.

'In answer to your earlier question, Matthew, you'll see that in Question 4 you're asked to describe what one of the mine entrances looks like.' The schoolmaster turned his head and looked up at the dark opening in the hillside behind him.

'So we can climb up and have a look, sir?' Sam asked enthusiastically.

'Yes . . . when it's your turn. And I'll be with you keeping an eye on things. You can see from here that when the mine was worked out, they put a metal grill across to stop people going in.'

'You could easily get through that,' Kelsey pointed out.

'Exactly!' Mr Duder said firmly. 'And that's why you're not going near unless I'm there. Is that understood?'

Everyone nodded solemnly.

Miss Dingle stood up. 'OK . . . you're to work in pairs. Calum and Billy . . . no doubt you two would like to work together?'

The two friends nodded.

'Harry . . . you can go with David. OK?

'Fine, miss,' both boys agreed.

'And I think we'll put the two troublemakers together . . . Matt and Sam.'

'Double trouble!' Mr Duder quipped. 'I'll really have to keep my eye on you two.'

'What about you, Kelsey? Who would you like to go with?'

'Put her with Humph, miss.' Sam shouted. 'I know she'd *love* to go with him!'

Everyone laughed out loud . . . except Oliver . . . who, by the look on his face, failed to see the funny side of Sam's suggestion.

'We'll let the three girls work together and Ollie can go with Craig. Then we're all sorted. How's that?' Miss Dingle asked cheerfully.

'OK, guys!' Mr Duder said. 'See how you get on and take your time, we're not in any rush.'

Billy looked at his clipboard and read Question 1:

'What precious metal were the miners digging for here in the late 19th century?'

He looked at Calum. 'Gold, I suppose,' Billy said. 'What do you reckon?'

'No . . . it was lead. Dude mentioned it in his spooky story . . . when we were sat around the fire.'

Billy nodded and wrote the answer in the space provided.

He read Question 2:

'Can you see any metal rails on the ground? What metal are they made of and what were they used for?'

'Mmmm . . . two questions in one,' Billy muttered. 'Well . . . at least I can see the metal rails. They're here – at the side of us.'

Calum looked to their left. Sure enough, two parallel rusted rails ran away from them towards the base of the limestone cliff, directly beneath the mine entrance up on the hillside.

'Railway lines!' Billy said confidently. 'Definitely railway lines . . . to carry the lead . . . in some sort of wagons, I suppose.'

'You're right,' Calum said, chewing the end of his pencil. 'And the rails are made of iron . . . that's why they're rusted.'

The two friends filled in their answers. A quick glance around showed that the other Year 7s were engrossed in doing the same.

Finally Billy and Calum reached the last question. It was in two parts:

In your own words, describe the entrance to one of the old mines.

Why do you think the miners wore thick woollen garments, even during the summer months?'

Both boys looked around for Mr Duder. It seemed that the schoolmaster had already scrambled up the rocky path to the mine entrance.

'Can we come up, sir?' Calum called up to him.

'And me, sir!' Oliver called up.

'And me!' Craig Green joined in.

Mr Duder called down to them. 'Billy and Calum . . . you two first. Oliver and Craig after that. I only want two at a time.'

Billy felt his heart race as he and Calum set off up the steep limestone path. This was the sort of schoolwork Billy liked . . . so much better than being stuck in a classroom back at school . . . but the nervous feeling was still plaguing his stomach.

'Take your time, you two,' Mr Duder called down. 'No rush!'

A few seconds later the two boys were alongside the schoolmaster on a wide ledge. As he scribbled notes on a clipboard of his own, Billy and Calum peered through the twisted metal bars into the eerie blackness of the cave opening.

'Blimey, that looks scary in there!' Calum uttered.

Billy followed his gaze. At first he couldn't see anything, but as his eyes accustomed themselves to the darkness, he saw that the floor of the cave had a large hole in it . . . about three or four metres beyond the entrance. Poking his head through the bars and peering down into the dark void, he saw a large clump of ferns sprouting from the vertical limestone walls.

The schoolmaster looked up from his clipboard, 'Not too close, Billy! We don't want any accidents.'

The hole looked deep . . . bottomless. 'Those ferns down there look like giant spiders webs,' Billy mused.

'Mmmm . . . very poetic,' Mr Duder smiled. 'Have you noticed anything else?'

Calum answered for him, 'There's some sort of hook and chain hanging down from the roof, sir – right above the hole. I suppose that was used to hoist up the lead.'

'Good thinking, Calum. But you're wrong. It was used to hoist a metal cage up and down the shaft. Can you guess what was in the cage?'

Calum followed Billy's example and poked his head through the metal bars, 'Miners, sir. But it must have been a small cage. The hole doesn't look that big.'

'The "hole" as you call it, is a "shaft". Mines running

downwards are called "shafts" and those running horizontally are called "drifts". And you're right – the cage only carried two miners at a time.'

Calum stepped back, sat on the ground and looked at his clipboard. Billy followed his example.

Why do you think the miners wore thick woollen garments, even during the summer months?'

Billy was just thinking about the answer when a noise from inside the mine drew his attention. Mr Duder and Calum also heard it. The three of them looked towards the entrance.

'Nothing to worry about,' Mr Duder said reassuringly. 'Probably just some loose stones.'

Billy crept up to the metal grill and crouched low.

A current of cold air whistled out from the mine and caused him to shiver. Now he realised why the miners wore warm clothes, even in summer.

'I bet it's freezing in there, sir. Is that why they wore thick clothes and stuff?'

The schoolmaster nodded enthusiastically. 'I'm impressed, Billy. Put it down on your sheet.'

Calum also looked impressed. Billy felt good. Sometimes even *he* could be clever!

Another noise in the mine caused Billy to look up from his clipboard. It was only a slight noise and this time it seemed only he had heard it. He grabbed the metal bars in both hands and poked his head through. As his eyes penetrated deep into the void, he saw the outline of something crouching in the darkness . . . just beyond the deep shaft. It was too dark to see clearly, but the shadowy form looked dog-like . . . and yet it was sitting up on two legs . . . almost human!

*Billy's heart turned to ice as the sinister shape retreated
back into the darkness and disappeared from view.*

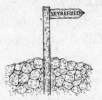

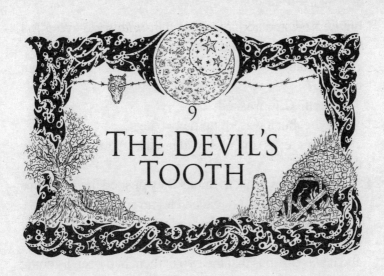

9
THE DEVIL'S TOOTH

The rest of the morning passed without incident.

The Year 7s worked their way through the questions on their clipboards and finally broke for lunch. They talked excitedly about the mineshaft entrance up in the hillside; the news had got around that Billy had seen some sort of animal hiding there.

Billy and Calum tucked into the packed lunches they'd help prepare earlier.

'Did you *really* see something in there? Could it have been a trick of the light?'

Billy took a bite from his cheese and tomato roll and replied with his mouth full, crumbs spluttering everywhere, 'No way! I really saw something! It nearly gave me a heart attack!'

Calum was about to take a bite from his own sandwich,

but he hesitated and looked at Billy with wide eyes, 'Tell me again what it looked like.'

'Like some sort of animal . . . similar to a dog . . . but bigger!'

'A wolf?' Calum asked.

'Maybe, but it was sat up on two legs.'

Calum's eyes opened wider still, 'You don't really think . . .'

'I don't know what to think!' Billy pushed the rest of his roll into his mouth and reached for an apple.

A voice sounded from behind them, 'Oooohhh . . . Billy saw the Moonwailer!' It was Sam, sitting with Matthew, and it was obvious that the two of them had been listening in to Billy and Calum's conversation. 'It's funny . . . but we didn't see a thing,' he added.

'No . . . neither did anyone else,' Matthew joined in. 'Seems to me, Billy, that you've been overdoing it on the imagination front. Probably been watching too many scary DVDs!'

'No way!' Calum said on Billy's behalf. 'If Billy said he saw something . . . then he saw something! In any case, this is a private conversation . . . so keep your big noses out!'

Billy laughed and took a huge bite from a crunchy apple. Sam and Matthew sighed and looked away.

'It makes sense,' Billy said, continuing more quietly than before. 'I told you we were being watched. That werewolf . . . or whatever it is . . . is probably watching us right now . . . sitting here . . . scoffing our lunch.'

Calum looked around nervously. 'Do you really think so?'

Billy replied with a grave nod of his head. 'We need to

be on full alert.'

The two friends scanned around the limestone scenery and discussed how easy it would be for someone - or something - to spy on them. They began to feel very uneasy.

As soon as lunch was finished, Mr Duder addressed everyone. 'Right then! Make sure you pick up all your litter and put it in the plastic bag that Craig is bringing round and then we'll be on our way.'

Ten minutes later everything was cleared and the school party was ready to move on. Billy and Calum pulled on their rucksacks and joined the others assembled by the gate at the top end of the mine site.

'Where are we going next, sir?' Kelsey asked expectantly.

'Well we're not going near any shops!' Sam teased.

'You are *so* not funny!' Kelsey snapped back. 'In any case . . . I wasn't talking to you, so keep your big . . .'

'OK! That's enough!' Miss Dingle interrupted. 'Let's hear what Mr Duder has to say.'

The schoolmaster continued, 'Well . . . we're going to carry on in a northerly direction along the footpath. . . just for a short distance . . . and then we'll round the top edge of that hill over there . . .'

'Black Hill,' Oliver reminded them.

Mr Duder nodded. '. . . Until we come across a tall rock formation. I think you'll find it quite interesting.'

'Is that the "Devil's Tooth", sir?'

'Right again, Ollie,' Mr Duder said. 'It used to be called the "Standing Stone".'

Some of the party looked intrigued, others less interested.

'Anyway . . . we're *all* going to take a look at it,' Mr Duder said firmly.

'And then what?' Kelsey asked impatiently.

Mr Duder folded his arms. 'Once we've had a look at the stone, we'll return to the campsite in a southerly direction along a parallel footpath on the far side of Black Hill.'

'Is that meant to sound exciting, sir?' Kelsey asked.

'It *is* exciting!' Oliver interrupted loudly. 'We'll be heading back through Howling Ghyll.'

'So what's so special about that?' Shannon asked, shrugging her shoulders as she spoke.

'It's haunted!'

The Year 7s fell silent and stared at Humph.

'By that Moonwailer thing that you keep going on about?' Sam asked with a curious grin on his face.

Humph nodded and looked indignant. 'I wasn't aware that I was going on about it! You lot keep asking questions . . . I just keep supplying the answers!'

'Once again, Ollie is right,' Mr Duder said, fastening his rucksack as he spoke. 'The ghyll is reputedly haunted by the young werewolf I told you about.'

'With eyes the size of dishes, sir, to quote from the guidebook.'

'That's right, Ollie. But it's just local superstition . . . a legend . . . a myth . . . nothing for us twenty-first century folk to worry about.'

As the schoolmaster spoke, Billy felt the butterflies fluttering in his stomach again. It was too much of a coincidence . . . the feeling of being watched . . . seeing something hiding in the mineshaft . . . *and now talk of the legendary Moonwailer!*

*

Once through the top gate Miss Dingle and the Year 7s followed Mr Duder in a single line along the footpath, which finally veered off to the right and made its way around the far side of Black Hill. As they rounded a bend, they reached the edge of a grassy clearing. In the centre a tall stone stood out clearly.

Kelsey sat down on a boulder and complained about her feet . . . how they were aching . . . how a blister had formed on one of her heels. Most of the other Year 7s were taken up at the sight of the curious rock.

Matthew pointed at it. 'Wow! It looks just like . . .'

'. . . A devil's tooth!' Sam finished for him. 'It's sort of tall . . . and sharp . . . and . . . pointed!'

Mr Duder stood with his hands on his hips, 'It must be about four metres high.'

'Can we go over and have a closer look?' Matthew asked.

The schoolmaster smiled. 'Course you can . . . but don't go climbing on it.'

Billy stood rooted to the spot, scanning the rock from top to bottom. The stone looked mysterious to say the least. It stood out from its surroundings so much that it looked as if it shouldn't even be there.

A few of the boys had already run over to the side of the stone. Craig was examining the base. 'There's some letters and numbers carved here,' he remarked.

Matthew stood with his hands on his hips, straining his head to see to the top. 'I'd love to have a go at climbing to the top,' he said fearlessly. 'My Uncle Josh's a climber. He'd do it easily.'

Craig ignored him and continued staring at the carvings. 'I think they're initials.'

Billy and Calum went over with Mr Duder to have a look.

'Look! "J.K. 1851-61",' Craig said.

Mr Duder scratched the back of his head. 'Mmmm . . . that's very interesting.'

Calum nudged Billy and the two of them walked away to the edge of the clearing. 'Do you still think we're being watched?' Calum whispered.

Billy nodded and scratched his head. He was staring at a large bowl-like depression in the ground just a few metres from where they were standing. Tall grass and nettles covered the surface of the hole. He estimated it to be about three to four metres across.

'What do you think that is?'

Calum shrugged his shoulders. 'No idea.'

Mr Duder walked up behind them. 'It's an old mine-shaft. Sometimes the miners just dug holes into the ground and then lowered themselves down. You'll find loads of them around and about. They've all been filled in now, and as you can see, they're completely overgrown.'

Billy and Calum nodded and gazed around. Mr Duder was right . . . there were more of the strange circular holes scattered around the clearing.

'They look weird,' Billy said.

'Like they've been made by aliens,' Calum added.

A sudden movement caught Billy's eye. He saw something on the hillside, just to his right.

Meanwhile, back at the Devil's Tooth, Matthew had ignored Mr Duder's instructions and had climbed almost to the top of the tall rock. The other boys cheered. Billy heard them, but took no notice. He was too preoccupied staring up at the limestone scar where the top of Black Hill met the skyline.

There it was again . . . a definite movement in the shadow of a clump of twisted trees sprouting out from the top of the chalk face.

'I THOUGHT I TOLD YOU NOT TO CLIMB ON THAT ROCK!' Mr Duder's voice boomed out.

Matthew was now perched on top of the tooth-shaped rock. He began howling like a wild dog and the other boys roared with laughter. Calum turned towards them and started laughing.

But Billy wasn't laughing. He saw the fast-moving shadow again, this time racing through the twisted trees.

'GET DOWN!' the schoolmaster bellowed.

Billy turned and looked at Matthew, still perched there, howling even louder and enjoying the other boys' attention. At the same time a large lump of limestone hurtled out of nowhere and struck the top of rock pillar, just below the boy's feet.

'Hey! Who threw that?' Matthew asked incredulously.

Everyone looked around at each other as Matthew started to climb down.

A second lump of rock, bigger than the first, struck Matthew on the foot.

'OUCH! WHO DID THAT!?'

As Matthew clambered back to the ground the other boys backed away.

'IT'S SOMEONE UP THERE!' Billy cried out, his eyes now glued to the steep limestone slope.

Everyone looked towards the clump of twisted trees where Billy was staring.

Another lethal missile struck the ground.

'Mr Duder cried out, 'GET AWAY FROM THERE!'

The Year 7s gawped at the heavy rock that had just struck the ground. Only Billy continued to stare upwards. He saw something move back into the shadows of the trees.

The group retreated and reassembled well away from the tall stone. All of the boys looked shaken. Matthew was extremely quiet.

'Are you alright?' Miss Dingle asked, putting an arm around Matthew's shoulder. 'Mr Duder told you not to climb on the stone. Why can't you do as you're told? Still . . . I can't believe anyone would throw stones at you like that.'

'I can!' Billy said quietly to Calum. 'Someone . . . or *something* . . . up there.' He fixed his gaze on the trees at the top of the limestone cliff.

'But why?' Calum asked, shaking his head.

'I don't know,' Billy whispered. 'But I'm sure I saw something . . . it's probably watching us right now. The sooner we're away from here, the better!'

Almost as if in response to Billy's comment, Mr Duder began to speak. 'OK! Let's move. Someone's playing silly beggars and I'm in no mood to find out who it is! I think we should get back to the campsite as quick as we can.' The schoolmaster forced a smile. 'In any case, I don't know about anyone else, but I'm starving. Once we're back at the campsite, we'll set about preparing a good meal.'

Kelsey was still sitting on a rock. She'd taken one of her boots off and Miss Dingle was helping her to stick a plaster over her blister. 'That's the best news I've heard in ages,'

Kelsey said.

The schoolmaster smiled again, but Billy saw the worried look in his eyes.

'Are we still going back through Howling Ghyll, sir?' Oliver asked in his usual matter-of-fact way.

'Oh . . . pleeeeease, sir!' Sam begged. 'We want to see the . . . Moon . . . thing.'

'The "Moonwailer",' Oliver corrected him.'

'That's right, sir. The Moonwailer. The werewolf with eyes the size of . . . fishes!'

Oliver sighed. '. . . dishes!'

'That's it . . . dishes!'

The other boys laughed. The girls laughed. Even Miss Dingle giggled a little. But Billy sensed that most of the laughter was of the nervous kind. The flying lumps of limestone had unsettled everyone.

Mr Duder forced yet another smile. 'OK . . . let's go. We'll head for the ghyll. It's the quickest route back.'

A few of the Year 7 boys cheered. The girls said nothing. Billy and Calum remained quiet.

'Are you OK, Billy?' Calum asked as he slipped his rucksack on.

'No!' Billy replied. 'I'm *not* OK. There's trouble ahead . . . I can feel it!'

Calum gawped at him. 'This Moonwailer thing! You don't honestly think it's real, do you?'

Billy pulled on his own rucksack. He looked back at Calum and saw the fear in his eyes. 'Yes, I do. And I think it's been watching us for ages. In any case, those rocks thrown at Matty didn't just come out of nowhere. They were real enough!'

Calum nodded silently.

As they walked over to rejoin the other Year 7s, something caught Billy's attention again. He looked over his shoulder. A flurry of loose stones cascaded down from the base of the clump of trees up on the hillside. His heart began to beat faster.

There was no doubt in his mind that something was stalking them. It was making its way down the hillside and about to follow their trail.

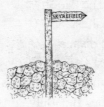

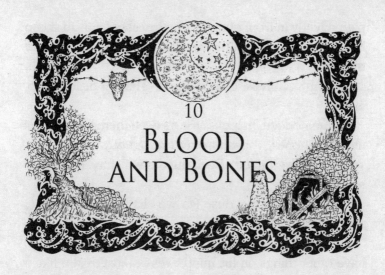

10

BLOOD
AND BONES

Mr Duder led the school party away from the Devil's Tooth and on past the edge of the grassy clearing until the footpath appeared again. After a short distance it forked left and right. They watched as the schoolmaster consulted his map.

'OK. We turn right here and head down the opposite side of Black Hill. This way!'

Billy and Calum followed directly behind Mr Duder, leading the line of pupils. As they walked on, everyone looked around anxiously, checking that the 'stone thrower' was nowhere in sight. But all was quiet. Nothing stirred.

The footpath was easygoing. It skirted Black Hill and descended gently towards the environs of Howling Ghyll.

Billy was the first to see the log fence crossing the footpath directly in front of them. The carcass of a dead sheep hung from a couple of rusty nails sticking out from one of the logs.

'Ughhh . . . gross!' Billy whined. 'That's a dead sheep, isn't it?'

Calum nodded, 'It looks as if it's been there for ages. It's nearly all bones . . . apart from a few bits of wool.'

'And I don't think it's been put there by travellers!' Billy said.

Calum looked nervous. 'Do we climb over the fence, sir?' he asked.

Mr Duder barely noticed the dead animal. He seemed to have other things on his mind. 'Yes . . . just treat it like a stile. This path isn't a public footpath; it's what they call a "permitted right of way".'

Billy didn't understand what was meant by a 'permitted right of way', but he did understand that that they were allowed to cross over the fence. Right now though he wasn't sure whether that was a good idea or not!

With Miss Dingle taking up the rear, the pupils clambered easily over the barrier and entered into the narrow gorge. As the steep sides of the ghyll closed in, a buzz of anticipation rippled through the party, some still wincing at the sight of the rotting sheep, some discussing it excitedly.

'WOOF! WOOF! GRRRR!'

'OK, Sam . . . that's quite enough!' Miss Dingle's voice rang out from somewhere behind.

The Year 7s laughed . . . apart from Billy and Calum. The two friends had already encountered enough spooky goings on in their lives to make them take things more seriously.

A little further on, the footpath became a dried up stream bed and a gnarled and twisted tree sprouted from its rocky base, almost barring their way. It gave Billy the impression of an obstacle, put there to keep people out . . . or perhaps to keep something in!

The light suddenly changed . . . it went dark and turned more gloomy. Billy looked up and saw a huge black cloud hanging over them, obscuring the sun. At the same time a cool wind whistled along the limestone gorge making an eerie moaning sound.

'Blimey! It's getting spooky!' Calum said quietly.

'I know!' Billy said in a whisper. 'I'm getting really bad vibes. I feel like there's something's waiting for us . . . up ahead.'

'But I thought it was following us,' Calum said in a shaky voice.

Billy glanced up at the steep sides of the ravine. 'It was . . . but it could have gone past us now. It might be waiting to ambush us!'

Mr Duder turned and shouted to the back of the line, 'OK? Is everyone keeping up?'

'We're all here!' Miss Dingle replied from the rear.

'Right! Just keep in line and keep together!' Mr Duder ordered. 'Watch where you're putting your feet – there are rocks and sharp stones everywhere. You'll need to squeeze past this old tree – it's a tangle of sharp branches – don't catch yourself on it. And watch out for loose rocks rolling down the sides of the ravine. Keep your eyes and ears open!'

'Apart from that, it's as safe as houses!' Sam shouted sarcastically.

A few of the pupils laughed. But most of them stayed

silent and gazed nervously ahead . . . especially Billy and Calum.

Mr Duder edged carefully past the tree and Billy and Calum did the same. They walked on a little further before stopping and waiting for the rest of the line to catch up.

A scream of pain reached their ears.

'WHAT'S HAPPENED?' Mr Duder shouted.

'It's Martine!' Miss Dingle called back. 'She caught her face on one of the tree branches.'

Billy and Calum and everyone else gathered around Martine. Blood trickled from a cut just under her right eye. Miss Dingle sat her down on a large rock and dabbed at it with a handkerchief. Tears trickled down Martine's cheeks.

'Don't worry!' Mr Duder reassured her. 'We'll soon have you sorted.'

The schoolmaster dug deep into his rucksack and brought out a small cloth bag with a green cross on it – a first aid kit. While he attended to Martine's injury, Billy looked ahead. The ravine appeared even more dark and mysterious.

'Right, Martine . . . it's not a deep cut. More of a scratch. That dressing should keep it clean until it heals up.'

'Thanks, sir!' Martine said meekly.

Billy looked at her tear-stained face and felt sorry for her.

Miss Dingle tossed back her hair and smiled broadly, 'She'll be fine. I'll keep her close to me.'

The schoolmaster nodded and resumed his place at the front of the line. The party moved on.

The way ahead became more difficult. The sides of the ravine grew steeper and closed in. The dried up stream bed became strewn with large rocks and fallen chunks of limestone.

Billy and Calum picked their way through it and kept close to Mr Duder.

'Wow! Look! Another cave . . . just up there!' Sam said as he caught up with them. 'Can we go up and have a look, sir?'

Mr Duder stopped and sat on a big limestone boulder. Billy saw that he was slightly red in the face and was breathing heavily. The cave that Sam had spotted was only a short climb up to their left.

'OK! We'll take five and let the stragglers at the back catch up. You can go and have a quick look, Sam. *But don't go in it!* Matthew! You stay here. I'm not sure I can trust you any more.'

Matthew frowned and sat on a rock.

Sam shot up the side of the ravine like a wild rabbit. 'Come on, you two . . .' he shouted down to Billy and Calum. 'Come and have a look. You never know . . . we might find a werewolf!'

The two friends followed cautiously.

As Sam reached the cave entrance, he crouched in front of it and took a torch from his rucksack. Lower down the slope Billy pulled on Calum's shoulder and stopped him.

'What's wrong?' Calum asked nervously.

At first Billy said nothing. He stood as still as a statue and gazed up at the skyline. He sniffed the air like some wild creature and strained his ears.

'What is it?' Calum repeated.

'There's something up there!'

As Billy spoke, a piercing shriek rang out from just above their heads. Everyone below froze and looked up as Sam stumbled backwards from the cave entrance and rolled down the rocky slope. He clung onto his torch – it was still lit, but the glass smashed as he hit the bottom.

Mr Duder jumped up and ran towards him. 'NOW WHAT?'

A very shaky Sam picked himself up and an even shakier Mr Duder began dusting him down. Billy and Calum scrambled back down and rushed to help.

'What happened?' Mr Duder repeated.

Billy looked at Sam's face. It was pale . . . his eyes stricken with fear. He could hardly speak.

'In . . . inside the cave . . .' He pointed upwards. 'There's . . . there's . . . something just inside the entrance . . . it's gruesome!'

Some of the other boys ran over, 'Crikey . . . what did you see?' someone asked.

Sam continued to stutter, '. . . bb . . . blood . . . and . . . bb . . . bones. Some sort of dead body. It's gross!'

'Watch him, will you, Miss Dingle?' Mr Duder said as the rest of the party caught up. 'I'd better go and investigate.'

Miss Dingle nodded solemnly.

'We'll go with you, sir,' Billy and Calum said together. The schoolmaster didn't reply. He was already struggling up towards the cave. The two friends scrambled up after him.

By the time Billy and Calum reached the cave, Mr Duder was crouched by the entrance holding a handkerchief over his nose. Aware of an awful stench, Billy and Calum put their hands over their noses and peered warily over his shoulder. 'What is it, sir?' Calum asked in frightened expectation.

Mr Duder switched on his torch and shone its powerful

beam into the cave entrance.

The three of them jumped backwards . . . overcome by the awful sight that greeted their eyes.

'It's the remains of a dead ram. It's not a pretty sight.'

Billy took a deep breath and peered once again over the schoolmaster's shoulder. He almost choked at the sight of the dismembered corpse. The ram's head was completely detached from its body, its eyes staring lifelessly into Mr Duder's torch beam. One of its front legs had been ripped off and was lying by its head. But the worst thing of all was that the ram's torso was ripped into shreds . . . a mass of blood and pulpy flesh . . . as if something had been tearing into it. There were also a number of bones and a few sheep skulls littered around the cave. No wonder Sam had fallen backwards!

'Blimey . . . what could have done that, sir?' Calum asked the shocked schoolmaster.

'I don't know,' Mr Duder said, pulling the boys away from the entrance. 'Probably some kind of dog . . . maybe the one the police warned us about. This could be its lair.'

'But a dog wouldn't be able to drag a full-size ram up here, sir?' Calum pointed out.

Mr Duder didn't reply. He looked thoughtful.

Billy's spine tingled as he thought about the legendary Moonwailer. Did the werewolf creature really exist? Was Dude thinking the same thing?

The rain started up and interrupted Billy's train of thoughts. First just a few big drops . . . and then it began to pour. 'We'd better get back to the others, sir.' Billy said. 'We're going to get soaked.'

The schoolmaster put his torch back into his rucksack and stood there, almost in a trance. Billy sensed what he was thinking. *What else could go wrong?*

As the three of them scrambled back down the rocky slope, a blood-curdling howl sounded from somewhere above them.

It was a howl of defiance, a howl of warning. It echoed around the ravine and caught on the edge of the moaning wind so that everyone heard it. All their hearts raced at the sound of it.

Billy and Calum stared at one another and tried to put on a brave face. *But neither of them could stop shaking.*

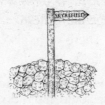

11
RACE FOR HOME

Mr Duder had taken the lead again and quickened his pace.

The wind gusted and the rain began to drive in, lashing into everyone's face. 'Don't dally at the back!' Mr Duder shouted over his shoulder. 'Keep together and move on quickly . . . we've dry tents waiting for us back at the campsite.'

Billy knew that it wasn't the rain that the schoolmaster was worried about. In any case, everyone was now wearing waterproofs. No . . . it was the series of bizarre events that had rattled Mr Duder. Billy was sure of it.

Since they'd heard the unearthly howling, the school party had pushed on with renewed urgency. Some of the Year 7s had started complaining – Craig was struggling to keep up with the pace and Kelsey's blister was rubbing against her boot – her pain increasing with every step.

Miss Dingle had pulled the hood of her waterproof tight around her face and taken her place at the rear. She uttered comments of encouragement to chivvy the back markers along, but it was obvious that she was just as nervous as everyone else.

'This is getting *seriously* scary!' Calum murmured.

Billy nodded. 'I know. The worst thing is not knowing whether that thing is in front of us or behind us.'

As the school party struggled on, the dried up stream bed became a tumble of larger boulders. They had no choice but to clamber over them, leaping from one to another, as if they were steppings-tones.

'I'm sorry about this!' Mr Duder cried over his shoulder. 'I didn't realise the going would be so tough. Watch your-selves! The rocks are slippery.'

In the same instant, Calum's foot slid off a boulder and he fell awkwardly, twisting his ankle. He sat on the stony ground, Billy beside him.

'Are you OK?' Billy asked.

'No . . . my ankle really hurts. I've twisted it.'

Mr Duder was so intent on moving forward he failed to hear Calum's cries and continued battling on down the ravine.

The wind howled louder, the rain drove in harder and everything turned darker. Billy stayed by Calum's side and looked around. He gawped at the sheer sides of the cliffs. They were now at their highest . . . hundreds of feet of limestone looming over them.

As the others caught up, they gathered around Calum.

'Now what's happened?' Miss Dingle asked anxiously.

Billy shouted through the rain, 'It's Calum, miss. He's

twisted his ankle.'

Miss Dingle eased through the Year 7s and knelt beside Calum. 'Where's Mr Duder?'

Everyone turned and looked ahead.

The schoolmaster had only just realised that there was no one following him and had turned back. 'WHAT'S WRONG?' he called out to them.

Billy sensed the anxiety in the schoolmaster's voice.

Sam shouted through cupped hands at the top of his voice, 'IT'S CALUM, SIR! HE'S TWISTED HIS ANKLE.'

They watched as the schoolmaster scrambled back towards them. He reached the huddle, took a look at Calum's ankle and confirmed that he'd twisted it . . . perhaps sprained it slightly. At least it wasn't broken. He rummaged in one of his anorak pockets and took out a mobile phone.

Billy glanced around. Some of the Year 7s had started shivering with cold and Kelsey winced with pain – her blister had burst. The weather was getting worse with every second . . . and to top everything . . . some sort of creature seemed to be following their progress. Billy realised the situation was getting serious. By the looks on the teachers' faces . . . they did too!

'I can't get a signal,' Mr Duder sighed, putting his mobile phone back in his pocket. 'The campsite's only about fifteen minutes away. Would you be happy to stay with Calum, Miss Dingle, while the rest of us go on and get help? Or *I'll* stay if you'd rather.'

'I think I'd better stay,' Miss Dingle said. 'You'll be much quicker than me.'

'I'll stay as well,' Billy said.

'Me too!' Kelsey added. 'My blister's killing!'

'How about you, Craig?' the schoolmaster asked, 'Do you think you can manage to keep up with us or would you rather stay and wait?'

Craig's voice trembled. 'I'll wait, sir. My asthma's coming on a bit.' He took an inhaler from his pocket and used it a couple of times.

Miss Dingle stood with her hood gathered tightly around her face, her hands deep in her pockets. Billy thought she looked like a small penguin. 'Fine! Try not to be too long . . . these kids are getting very cold . . . me too, for that matter.'

Matthew was already on his way, rapidly clambering over boulders and heading away down the ravine. 'Come on! Let's go for it!'

'Not so fast, Matthew!' Mr Duder shouted after him. 'I think I'd better take the front.' He turned back to Miss Dingle. 'Shouldn't be more than half an hour. Sure you'll be OK?'

'We'll be fine. Just go!' Miss Dingle said firmly. Billy saw the worry in her mascara-smudged eyes.

As Mr Duder and the others set off at a determined pace, Miss Dingle suggested that the remaining group should move over to the side of the ravine and shelter under the lea of the limestone cliff. It sounded a good idea. Anything to get out of the horrid weather.

Leaning on Billy, Calum managed to limp over to the steep wall of rock. Miss Dingle and the girls followed and before long they were all nestled under one of the many gnarled trees sprouting out from the limestone.

'It's a good idea sheltering under here, miss,' Billy said, trying to be positive. 'It'll keep the rain off and stop any loose rocks falling on us.'

Kelsey had taken her boot off again and was gently peeling the plaster back to expose her burst blister, 'Nice one, Billy,' she said in a cynical tone of voice. 'But that wasn't exactly the wind howling back there, was it? Who's going to protect us from that?'

With perfect timing Kelsey's question was answered by another blood-curdling cry. It rang out from somewhere above them. The sound hung on the wind and drifted away so slowly that it seemed to last forever.

They all sat stiffly in shocked silence.

'We'll be OK!' Billy said. 'As long as we stick together.'

Calum nodded. 'Billy's right. Safety in numbers and all that!'

Miss Dingle forced a smile. 'Mr Duder won't be long now.' She looked at her watch, 'They've already been gone ten minutes.'

Everyone nodded and muttered words of encouragement. Craig had got his breath back, but had turned a funny white colour and looked really scared.

Billy, continually on the lookout, glanced back up the ravine. A tight knot suddenly formed in his stomach. 'I think we should move on a bit, miss. It's getting cold sitting here.'

Calum stared at him. 'Don't be daft, Billy? You know I can hardly walk.'

Kelsey looked at Billy with a painful expression. 'You can move on if you want. But I'm not moving a muscle. My foot's done in!'

Miss Dingle said nothing.

Glancing back again, Billy tried to keep calm. He took a deep breath and stood up. 'We *have* to move on . . . we've no choice.'

'Billy! What's up? What are you talking about?' Calum asked with wide eyes.

'Are you deliberately trying to frighten us?' Miss Dingle asked sharply.

'Yeah! You're freaking us out, Billy! Give it a rest!' Kelsey snapped.

'*Please... trust me!*' Billy said in his most pleading sort of voice. 'Just get up slowly. No sudden movements. Try to act normally and follow me. Whatever you do . . . don't look back.'

Of course, that was the worst thing that Billy could have said.

They all immediately looked around and saw the distant shadowy shape. It was crouching on a large boulder about a hundred metres away. As soon as it became aware of their attention, it raised its head and snarled so loudly that the sound rumbled around the walls of the ravine. Everyone went rigid . . . as if turned to stone.

'My God! Wh . . . what is it?' Calum stammered.

As if in reply, the creature let out another spine-chilling growl . . . *and crept slowly towards them*.

12
BLIND PANIC

Despite Billy's instructions to keep calm, his companions panicked.

Kelsey abandoned the sock and boot she'd taken off and scrambled away in the direction that Mr Duder and the others had taken earlier. Craig followed.

Miss Dingle continued to stare at the distant creature. She retreated a few steps and fell onto her back. Billy and Calum dragged her up and pulled her in the direction of Kelsey and Craig.

'LET'S GET OUT OF HERE!' Miss Dingle yelled.

To everyone's horror, the creature continued edging forward, as if readying itself to strike. Miss Dingle, now firmly on her feet, helped Billy to support Calum, but his ankle was agonising, and they struggled to make progress.

Moments later, Billy braced himself and looked behind.

The creature had closed in. It suddenly stood erect and howled into the darkened sky. Billy's heart almost stopped. This was like no animal he'd ever seen!

'I think it's going to strike!' he cried out in a shaky voice.

'JUST KEEP GOING!' Miss Dingle yelled.

'We must . . . be nearly . . . at the end of the ravine,' Calum said in short gasps. He hopped desperately on one leg. 'Keep going, Billy. Stop looking behind!'

But Billy couldn't help himself . . . he continued to gaze back . . .

The creature was moving more quickly now, its features becoming clearer with every step.

To Billy it looked like a boy running on all fours, but the spine was too curved and the head wolf-like. He could see the long pointed ears quite clearly and the tufts of fur sprouting around the face. With fantastic agility it leapt from boulder to boulder, growling ferociously.

Billy was terrified and he shot forward, dragging Calum and Miss Dingle with him. 'Keep going! Keep going!' he yelled.

Kelly screamed up ahead. They looked towards her and saw that her path had been blocked by a hooded figure standing on a large rock.

'Who on earth is that?' Miss Dingle uttered.

'Quickly . . . get behind me!' the figure shouted. It was wearing some sort of trench coat and holding a long stick in its right hand.

'Don't look back! You'll be safe once you're in the water. Get over here . . . behind me!' the figure shouted.

The voice was deep – Billy guessed it was a man's.

'We've no choice!' Miss Dingle gasped. 'Do as he says!'

As they staggered on, the dried up stream bed suddenly

gushed with water. Kelsey and Craig shouted words of encouragement and within seconds, they were all gathered behind the strange figure, standing in the fast-flowing stream.

Billy looked back and saw to his relief that the advancing creature had stopped. It skulked behind a big boulder, just short of where the underground spring had sprouted, and peered accross at them.

'GET BACK! GO! LEAVE US IN PEACE!' their rescuer shouted.

The creature remained hidden, only its sinister shadowy head showing above the rock as it growled and snarled.

The hooded figure turned to the five members of the school party and pointed his stick towards a narrow opening at the base of cliff. 'Head over there . . . I'll be right behind you.'

Kelsey set off towards their escape route. The others followed, Craig breathing heavily again, Miss Dingle and Billy still supporting Calum, their rescuer taking up the rear.

Billy glanced back and saw that the hooded figure was walking with his back to them, holding his stick in a threatening way above his head.

At first their escape path was narrow and enclosed by steep cliffs. But as it climbed steeply, it widened out and quickly took them out of the ravine. Everyone kept glancing back – no one spoke. Five minutes later they found themselves standing high on a hillside, a wide green expanse stretching out before them, descending gently down to the valley bottom.

Their rescuer came up beside them. 'You're safer now.'

The rain was still lashing down and the man kept the hood of his waterproof tight around his face. Even so it was easy to see the scar under his left eye.

'We'll head down there, back to the house.' He lifted his stick and pointed down the hillside. Billy looked where he was pointing and saw the roof of a huge mansion sticking out from a clump of trees.

'Percival Hall' the man said calmly. 'Once the mansion house of a rich mine owner. Now it's a diocesan retreat.'

Billy gave the man a blank look.

The man smiled. 'It's a place where people come to have a bit of peace and quiet . . . to do a bit of thinking instead of rushing around all the time.'

'It looks a long way off,' Kelsey sighed.

The hooded man smiled again. 'Not as far as you think. You'll be safe there and we can get you dried out and sorted good and proper.'

Billy sighed with relief. Everyone offered their thanks. But Miss Dingle still looked worried. 'I don't mean to sound ungrateful, but we don't even know who you are . . .'

'Quite right! Quite right!' the man interrupted, allowing his hood to drop away from his face. 'My name's Boniface, Father Boniface. I'm a priest.'

Billy . . . and everyone else . . . stared at the man. The scar looked more prominent under his striking blue eyes.. His curly white hair, broad nose and square jaw made him look strong. Standing there in his long coat, with his stick held tightly in his right hand, he reminded Billy of a Roman emperor.

'There's another problem,' Miss Dingle went on. 'The rest of our school party went on ahead . . . to get help . . .'

'. . . I've twisted my ankle,' Calum informed him. 'It's really painful!'

'They'll probably be on their way back to us by now, miss,' Kelsey suggested.

'Have they got a mobile?' the priest asked.

'Yes, but Mr Duder couldn't get a signal,' Billy pointed out.

The priest lay his stick on the ground and took a mobile from a pocket in his coat. Billy wondered why he didn't put the stick in his other hand. 'I'll give it a go. At least I can get a signal up here. Now what's the number?'

Miss Dingle gave the priest the teacher's number and the priest managed to get through. Mr Duder and the other Year 7s had just set off with help. The priest spoke into his mobile for a little while longer and then switched it off. He put it back in his pocket and picked up the stick again . . . all with his right hand.

'OK, folks! Sorted!' The man who owns the campsite, David Jessop . . . I know him well . . . he's going to bring your schoolmaster and the others over to the hall. We can all dry out together and get acquainted. How does that suit you?'

Billy cheered inwardly. Kelsey cheered outwardly. Calum laughed and Craig's face gained some colour.

Miss Dingle held out an upturned palm . . . even the rain had stopped. She let down her hood, took a small hair-brush out of her pocket and brushed back her shoulder-length hair. 'What about Calum's ankle?'

The priest looked at Calum and frowned. 'OK, young man . . . let's have you!'

He crouched down and made to give Calum a piggyback . . . Calum needed no persuasion to take up the offer.

'That creature back there . . .' Billy started to ask.

'Let's get down to the hall,' the priest interrupted. 'I'm sure you've all manner of questions and I'll do my best to answer them when we're all warm and dry.'

The priest looked towards the teacher. 'Are we all ready, Mrs . . . ?'

'Dingle,' she said. '*Miss* Dingle.'

They trudged on down the hillside, Kelsey hobbling at the front with Craig just behind her, Father Boniface, with his stick in one hand, carrying Calum on his back and humming a tune, Billy and Miss Dingle trailing at the back . . . both deep in thought.

Billy had no doubt that their small party must have presented a strange sight to anyone who could see them.

After reaching the base of the hill and heading into the trees, they soon reached two impressive gateposts standing at the end of a long gravel drive. More black clouds closed in overhead and the rain threatened to start up again.

Father Boniface lowered Calum to the ground. 'Almost there! Just at the top of the drive. How's the ankle?'

Calum took a few steps. 'It still hurts . . . but not as bad. I think I can manage.'

He limped on alongside the others, their boots crunching over the gravel. The trees lining the drive dripped large drops of rainwater down onto them. Their feet squelched in wet boots from standing in the stream. No one bothered! They felt safer now and that was all that mattered.

Finally the avenue of trees opened up to reveal a huge Gothic-style mansion.

'Wow! This is even more spooky than the professor's house in Norfolk,' Calum gasped.

Billy nodded and stared at the building.

Two stone lions stood on sentry duty. The lions' faces were chipped and eroded, and like the stone steps leading up from them, dotted with lichens and moss, giving them an air of old age and antiquity.

He peered up at the great walls dotted with latticed windows, some rectangular, some arched . . . all with ornate stonework over the top of them. Some of the windows were lit with a dull sinister glow and Billy half expected to see faces peeping out from behind the laced curtains.

A vehicle crunched over the gravel behind them, snapping Billy back to the present. It was the rest of their party. Perfect timing!

Sam was first out of the four-wheel drive. 'Hi guys!' he shouted cheerfully.

The others piled out. Mr Duder was the last. He looked concerned. He walked over to Miss Dingle. 'Is everyone OK?'

'We are now!' Miss Dingle replied sharply.

David Jessop, driver of the Land Rover and owner of the campsite, walked over to the priest. Billy watched as they engaged in quiet conversation. The Year 7s chatted excitedly, everyone trying to speak at the same time.

A few minutes later Mr Jessop waved a cheery goodbye and instructed Mr Duder to phone if he needed any more help. The priest waved him off before leading everyone up the stone steps towards a pair of impressive carved doors. Billy took a deep breath and looked back at one of the stone sentries; half expecting to see the lion turn its head and stare back!

The priest rang the bell and an elderly woman wearing jeans and sweater, her hair as white as snow, appeared almost instantly. She greeted them with a smile.

'Hi, Agnes. I've brought visitors,' Father Boniface informed her.

'Well you'd better come in, all of you.'

The priest ushered them in and through into a large entrance hall.

'Agnes . . . would you take them down to the drying room?'

Agnes nodded and smiled. The priest turned towards the schoolteachers. 'You can hang all your wet things up in there. After that we'll meet back in the library.' He looked at Calum and Kelsey. 'And how about the two invalids? How are the ankle and the blister faring?'

'No problem,' Calum replied. 'I can put my weight on it now.'

'Well my blister's still killing, and . . .' Kelsey started.

'I'll sort that out,' Miss Dingle interrupted. 'It just needs a new plaster.'

'I'll bring you one,' Agnes smiled.

'That's OK then,' Father Boniface continued. 'I'll see you all in the library. There'll no doubt be a roaring fire waiting and if we ask Agnes kindly I'm sure she'll rustle up some hot drinks and biscuits.'

A ripple of anticipation spread through the Year 7s. Agnes smiled at the two teachers and led everyone off. She took them through a large ornate dining room and on past a kitchen and down a dingy corridor. They entered a small room with some sort of boiler in it. The room was very warm and had lots of hooks hanging from its walls. Several bits of clothing hung from the hooks, but most were empty.

'There you are!' Agnes said cheerily. 'You can hang your wet things up in here and they'll be dry before you go.' She rubbed her slender hands together as she spoke.

Billy looked carefully at the lady's face. It was an old face, lined and wrinkled, but Billy sensed the energy and kindness in her sharp hazel eyes.

'Now . . . if you'll all follow me . . .'

Talking in quiet whispers, they followed the old lady back through the dining room and on past the entrance where they'd gathered earlier. She led them down a panelled corridor with a strong smell of polish. They passed a couple of people who smiled at them, and on through a pair of impressive double doors at the end.

. . . And there was Father Boniface, standing with his back towards a roaring fire. The long trench coat and waterproof hood had gone and he looked altogether more normal, wearing a woollen sweater and baggy cord trousers. He smiled warmly at them as they filed in.

But Billy's eyes went straight towards the priest's left hand. He held it behind his back. Billy's curiosity grew further. *Why did he keep hiding it?*

'Now I want you all to make yourselves at home. Find somewhere comfy to sit and Agnes will be back shortly with refreshments.'

'Thank you,' Kelsey said loudly. She glanced at the teachers as she spoke. Billy guessed she was just trying to make an impression.

For the next few minutes, the Year 7s relaxed, chatted and glanced around the ornate room. Oliver Wright-Humphries buried his face in a book he'd brought with him.

Mr Duder stood up and walked over to the fire. He

stretched his hands out to warm them and looked at Father Boniface, 'Thanks for all this! We had quite an ordeal out there.'

'Some of us worse than others!' Miss Dingle said, clasping her hands together.

'Why don't you tell me what happened,' the priest suggested.

Billy noticed that his smile disappeared as he spoke.

'Can *I* tell him, sir?' Sam asked.

'I suppose so,' Mr Duder replied.

Agnes arrived with a trolley stacked with tea, hot chocolate and biscuits. 'Well before you get started, let's fix you up with something to eat and drink. We'll be polite and sort the teachers out first . . . what'll you two be having?'

As Agnes served drinks and biscuits, the fire suddenly made a loud crack. It sounded like a pistol shot and everyone jumped.

'Don't worry,' the priest said reassuringly. 'Just a damp bit of wood on the fire.'

As he spoke, he turned towards the flames. Billy's eyes shot straight towards his left hand, which he was still holding behind his back . . . *and then he glimpsed the shiny metal for the first time and knew immediately why the old priest preferred to keep it hidden.*

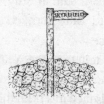

13
TRUTH
AND LIES

Sam told Father Boniface exactly what had happened . . . but in his usual rather haphazard way. '. . . And then me and the other guys, but not Calum or Billy, or Kelsey and Craig, went off with Dude . . . er . . . I mean Mr Duder . . .'

The Year 7s laughed out loud.

'. . . And got the farmer to help. But Dude . . . er . . . sorry, sir . . . Mr Duder . . . got a phone call . . . and we came straight here. And that's about it!'

'Well done, Sam!' Mr Duder said. 'That's pretty much what happened. But I believe things got a lot worse after that – at least for those who had to stay behind. Maybe one of the others could tell Father Boniface what happened after we left?'

'*I'll* tell him, sir!' Kelsey blurted out. Billy watched as some of the boys nudged each other and murmured their disapproval.

'Go on, Kelsey,' Miss Dingle said encouragingly.

'Well . . . after Dude's lot had gone . . .'

The Year 7s bellowed with laughter as Mr Duder sipped his tea and sighed.

'...Well, my foot was killing. I've got this blister, see... and...'

'OK! We know all about the blister,' Miss Dingle intervened. 'Just keep it brief and to the point.'

'Well, while we were sitting there, under a tree, Billy turned a bit freaky.' All eyes turned to Billy. 'So anyway . . . Billy said we should get up and move away . . . slowly like. Well . . . me and Calum asked him what he was on about . . . 'cause both our feet were killing. But Billy just kept on telling us to get up and move. And then he got *really* weird. He said not to look behind.'

'So what did you do?' the priest asked.

Kelsey took a sip of her drink. 'We looked behind!'

'And what did you see?' Matthew called out.

Everyone went deadly silent and waited for Kelsey's reply. '*I think it was a werewolf!*'

Mr Duder almost dropped his cup and saucer and Miss Dingle started a coughing fit. But Billy noted that Father Boniface showed no surprise.

'And that's where I came in,' the priest said solemnly. 'It's lucky I turned up and got you away from the beast.' He took a sip from his mug and smiled towards Kelsey. 'You'll be relieved to know, young lady, that the beast you saw was no werewolf.'

'Well what was it?' Calum asked impatiently. 'It scared the wits out of us.'

'Canis Lupus,' the priest answered mysteriously. 'Better known as . . .'

'A timberwolf,' Oliver interrupted, looking up from his book.

'Trust Humph!' Calum muttered to Billy. 'A walking encyclopaedia!'

'Quite right, young man,' Father Boniface said, looking very impressed. 'A *Canadian* timberwolf . . . to be precise.'

Oliver nodded politely and went back to his book.

'It looked bigger than a wolf,' Billy said calmly, '. . . More like a small bear. I saw it stand up . . . on two legs. Surely a wolf wouldn't do that.' He looked straight at the priest to see his response.

Father Boniface smiled faintly, but his eyes looked troubled. 'Trick of the light, young fellow. It was probably lunging forward.'

'As well as that may be, Father,' Mr Duder spoke up. 'Why would there be a wolf in Howling Ghyll? Wolves aren't found in the wild any more. Not in this country, anyway!'

'Good point, Mr Duder, but there's a simple explanation. Records show that some years ago, a travelling circus visited Skipdale. Amongst the animals on show was a pair of wolves. It's my belief that one of them escaped and took refuge out here in the wild.'

'Well why didn't the police warn us?' Mr Duder said. 'A wolf is much more dangerous than a stray dog. Haven't they heard of "risk assessment"?'

Father Boniface nodded gravely and continued. 'Despite it being sighted numerous times and being guilty of all sorts of misdemeanours . . . killing sheep and such . . . the police have never acknowledged its existence. A bit like the "Beast of Bodmin Moor" . . . it has given rise to all sorts of rumour and exaggeration. The police simply put it down to a stray. But they've never managed to catch it.'

'Well it doesn't seem very elusive at the moment,' Miss Dingle said. 'We only stepped out into the ghyll today and the wolf was straight onto us.'

The priest looked uncomfortable. He turned his back and stared into the fire. He spoke almost as if in a trance.

'You've been very unlucky. Normally the wolf runs at night . . . when darkness falls.'

Outside, a tree by the window bent over in the gusting wind; the end of one of its branches tapped on the glass making everyone jump around.

'Are wild wolves really dangerous?' Sam asked, his eyes wide with excitement. 'We saw what it did to a ram.'

Oliver looked up from his book again. 'A wolf will kill from instinct,' he stated in his usual matter-of-fact way.

Still staring into the fire, the priest continued. 'When I first arrived here I used to walk up the ghyll to the tall stone.'

'The Devil's Tooth,' Harry Meanwood intervened.

'Quite right! Sometimes I used to wander up there to meditate, especially on a nice day. But once I ventured up there late in the afternoon and the weather turned.'

'Was it dark?' Shannon asked, her voice beginning to tremble.

'Almost.'

'What happened?'

The priest turned to face them. 'The same thing that happened to you . . . the wolf followed me . . . stalked me.'

Calum fidgeted by Billy's side. 'And then what happened?'

'Fortunately . . . nothing! I made my way down the ghyll, as you did. The beast closed in, but I kept on going . . . hardly daring to look back . . . until I was back here.'

For the first time, the priest brought out his left arm and revealed his shiny metal wrist, complete with gleaming metal hook sticking out in place of his hand.

Everyone gasped . . . except Billy.

'Did the wolf do that?' Matthew asked.

Father Boniface smiled. 'It would make for a more exciting story, wouldn't it? But no . . . he didn't. The explanation is more simple . . . a car accident!'

A silence fell over the priest's audience. Everyone

stared at his lower arm. It was Calum who finally broke the spell, 'You said "he", Father Boniface.'

'Yes . . . I said "he" because the beast is a fully-grown male timberwolf.'

'Well . . . what about what happened to me?' Matthew reminded everyone. 'That was no wolf throwing lumps of rock back there . . . more like some "nutter" . . .'

'The "nutter" as you put it . . .' the priest interrupted, '. . . was more than likely one of the older children from Skyre-field . . . truanting from school. Not long ago a young lad had to be rescued from a mineshaft. They're always up to no good. Not much for them to do out here . . . they get bored!'

Billy stared hard at the priest's face. He sensed that he wasn't telling the truth. And then the priest looked back at him . . . and looked uncomfortable . . . as if he knew what Billy was thinking. For a few seconds that seemed like an eternity, Billy and the priest locked into each other's eyes . . . like some sort of showdown . . . until the priest turned away.

Billy knew immediately that his suspicions were correct . . . *the priest was lying!*

'In view of all that's happened, I'm thinking it might be best if we ended this activity trip and returned home,' Miss Dingle said, with a frown on her face.

The pupils muttered their disapproval and looked glumly towards Mr Duder.

The schoolmaster nodded, 'What with "risk assess-ment" and all the other red tape we teachers have to deal with, I'm inclined to agree with Miss Dingle. I'd no idea we'd be facing up to wolves out here.' He glanced around at the disappointed faces of the Year 7s. 'Your parents would be horrified if they knew what happened back there . . . and even worse . . . what *could* have happened!'

Billy felt disappointed and relieved at the same time.

Part of him wanted to delve deeper into the mystery surrounding the 'wolf', and part of him wanted to get as far away from Howling Ghyll as possible.

He looked at Father Boniface. The priest was staring at him again.

'No need to go home!' Father Boniface said without taking his eyes off Billy. 'Just keep away from Howling Ghyll. If you stay in the area south of the campsite, you'll be quite safe!'

'Mmmm . . . perhaps,' Mr Duder said, scratching his chin. 'I intended taking the Year 7s to Belton Priory tomorrow and I think that's south of here.'

The priest continued to stare at Billy. 'You're right, Mr Duder. And it's well worth a visit.'

'What about shops?' Kelsey chimed up. 'Are there any shopping centres near here?'

The boys groaned and the priest smiled, 'Belton Priory is a very interesting place. It dates back centuries . . . ran by Augustinian monks. It's got a café and . . .'

'. . . A shop?' Kelly interrupted.

The boys groaned again. 'We've come here to get away from all that,' Matthew said in a very mature sort of way.

'Oh shut up!' Kelsey snapped back at him. 'At least in shopping centres you wouldn't be bothered by wild animals . . . or timberdogs!'

Everyone burst out laughing. '*timberwolf!*' Oliver Wright-Humphries corrected her. '*Canadian timberwolf!*'

'Well . . . whatever!' Kelly snapped at him.

'What do you think?' Mr Duder asked, looking towards Miss Dingle.

The schoolmistress leaned forward in her chair and placed her hands on her lap. 'I'm still not sure!'

'*Please*, miss,' the pupils pleaded almost in one voice. 'We don't want to go home. Can we stay?'

'It's really cool and exciting being away from home,' Sam beamed.

'No one can argue about "exciting",' Miss Dingle frowned. 'Perhaps a bit too much excitement!'

'The enthusiasm of the young!' the priest said with a chuckle. 'It never fails to inspire me.'

'Well . . . if it's OK with Mr Duder . . . it's OK with me,' Miss Dingle said.

Mr Duder looked serious. 'We'll give it another day and see how we get on.'

A ripple of approval ran through the Year 7s.

Mr Duder continued, 'It's time we were off . . . back to the campsite. We've troubled Father Boniface quite enough for one day.'

'No problem at all, Mr Duder,' the priest smiled. 'I'll see you to the door. I think the worst of the weather has passed and it's only a short walk back to your campsite.'

Billy glanced over to the window. The tree branch that had earlier tapped on the pane was quite still. Thin rays of watery sunshine shone through the glass making a pattern on the carpet.

The priest walked out of the library followed by Mr Duder and Miss Dingle. Agnes appeared in the corridor outside. She led them back down to the drying room and helped them find their warm dry clothing. As the others filed out, Billy and Calum found themselves alone.

'What do you reckon to all this?' Calum whispered.

Billy answered quietly. 'I think that there's something really weird going on.'

'Me too!' Calum frowned. 'It's like you said . . . whenever we go away anywhere, you seem to attract trouble.'

'I know,' Billy sighed. 'Ghosts and spirits! And now were-wolves, maybe. Why me . . . what have I ever done?'

A voice from the doorway almost gave them a heart

attack. 'The Lord works in mysterious ways!' It was Father Boniface. He'd been standing outside the doorway and Billy guessed that he'd heard every word of their conversation.

The two boys looked at each other as the priest walked up to them.

'What's your name?' Father Boniface asked, smiling at Billy.

'Billy . . . Billy Hardacre.'

'And your friend?'

'Calum Truelove,' Calum answered.

The priest turned back to Billy. He smiled again and Billy saw the kindness in his eyes. 'We have something in common, Billy, you and I. We need to talk.'

'But . . . but . . . why? When?' Billy stammered.

'Don't worry. Just leave it to me. I'll get myself down to your campsite and we'll find a way to exchange a few words.'

'OK!' Billy whispered nervously. 'But just tell me one thing . . . that creature we saw . . . it wasn't a wolf was it?'

Father Boniface hesitated and looked towards the door. 'No, my son,' he said, with an expression of anxiety on his face, 'that was no wolf you encountered back there – it was a creature born of evil.'

'The . . . the . . . Moonwailer!' Billy stammered.

The priest nodded.

'So it *is* real . . .' Calum uttered.

The priest lifted his metal hand and pointed to the scar under his eye. 'Too true, young man . . . this was no car accident . . . *the Moonwailer is real!*

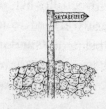

14
NIGHT CALLERS

By the time they had all returned to the campsite, everyone was ravenous. Miss Dingle and the girls immediately set about organising a super, slap-up feast. Billy overheard her telling Mr Duder that apart from feeding everyone's appetite, a good supper would take their minds off the scary events of the afternoon.

And what a supper it was!

Pre-cooked pizzas were warmed up and went down well – everyone ate at least two slices. There was also lots of healthier stuff . . . mixed salad, coleslaw and some jacket potatoes for those who were prepared to wait for them. Lots of bread – pita bread, thick-sliced wholegrain bread and plain white sliced bread for the less adventurous. There was a pan full of baked beans, another pan of tomatoes and a huge pan of creamed rice pudding for afters. Miss Dingle finally opened a large packet of chocolate biscuits to go with the drinks . . . tea, hot chocolate or Ovaltine.

Everyone tucked in and hardly spoke as they sat quietly emptying their plates. Never had a meal tasted so good!

And now Billy and Calum were snuggled up in their tent. They both lay on their backs, stretched out on their sleeping bags with hands folded over their full stomachs.

'Blimey . . . I'm bursting!' Calum groaned.

'Me too!' Billy said. 'I don't think I've ever eaten so much.'

Calum turned to face him and propped himself up on one elbow, 'I don't really feel like going to sleep. My mind's too active . . . even more active than my stomach!'

Billy looked at him, but remained on his back. 'I know what you mean. My mind's swirling.'

'Do you reckon that priest was telling the truth . . . about his arm? I mean, if he really was attacked by the Moon-wailer, then why did he go on and on about that Canadian timberwolf?'

'That was just a story to stop people being scared. I know he lied, but believe me . . . he's a good guy.'

'But how do you know?'

'I just do!' Billy said firmly.

A noise by the side of the tent and a small circle of light showing through the canvas made them both sit up. Calum shone his torch in the direction of the tent opening.

'OK, boys! Time for lights out. Goodnight.'

It was Mr Duder doing his rounds. Billy breathed a sigh of relief. 'Goodnight, sir!'

Calum followed his example, 'Goodnight!'

Calum crawled over to the tent entrance and checked it was closed with the zip fastener all the way to the bottom.

'It's shut . . . tight!' he muttered half under his breath.

Both boys lay back down again, this time with their hands behind their heads. Calum switched his torch off and all was in blackness. Billy stared hard, but he couldn't even see the roof of the tent. He closed his eyes and tried to relax. Thoughts of wolves, wild dogs, bears and werewolves swirled around in his mind. 'I'll never get to sleep,' he murmured.

'Same here!' Calum retorted. 'It's all getting spooky again . . . just like the last two "so-called" holidays!'

Billy recalled the sinister events of their Norfolk holiday. From the moment they'd arrived at the old windmill, danger had closed in on them. Same thing at Aunt Emily's – it was a miracle that he and Calum had survived! And now this camping trip seemed to be heading the same way.

The two friends talked about their 'Bonebreaker' and 'Dawn Demons' adventures and compared what had happened then to what was happening now. They chatted on in quiet whispers . . . until they finally drifted off to sleep.

When Billy awoke again, he'd no idea what time it was. He felt he'd only been asleep for a few minutes. Everything was still clothed in darkness. The wind had whipped up again; it gusted outside and caused the flysheet to make a flapping sound. He wondered if this was what had caused him to stir.

'Hi, Calum! Are you asleep?' Billy whispered, giving his friend a slight dig in the ribs.

Calum groaned and turned over. 'I *was*!'

'Sorry! It's just that I've got that uneasy feeling.'

Calum immediately sat up and faced him. He'd experienced enough of Billy's 'uneasy feelings' to know that they usually spelt trouble.

The wind gusted more strongly. The flysheet and the inner tent both flapped loudly. 'Blimey! It sounds wild out there,' Calum said, stretching his arms above his head.

Billy said nothing. He sat beside his friend and strained his ears. 'Sshhh . . . Somebody's coming!'

Calum's eyes opened wider. 'Naw . . . it's just the wind!'

Billy strained his ears even harder. 'I think I can hear someone moving about outside.'

Calum dug out his torch and grabbed his watch from underneath his pillow. He looked at it and turned to Billy. 'It's half-past two. Who'd be out there at this time of night?'

'I don't know . . . but surely you can hear it now? Sshhh . . . ! Listen!'

Sure enough, as the boys went quiet, the sound of approaching footsteps sounded outside the tent. Calum's expression turned to fear. 'WHO IS IT?' he called out.

Another circle of light showed through the canvas. But this time it was much too big to be torchlight. Billy's heart beat faster. By the look on Calum's face, his heart was racing too.

'I've just thought of something,' Billy said, trying to keep calm. 'The priest wanted to talk to me. Remember? Maybe it's him.'

'At this time! I don't think so!' Calum whispered, his voice trembling.

The circle of light moved round to the tent entrance. The two friends dived deeper into their sleeping bags and peered nervously towards the zipped opening.

They watched in terror as a long shadow appeared at the foot of the tent.

'I reckon it's one of the boys,' Calum said hopefully. 'Someone's playing tricks. It's got to be!'

'WHO IS IT?' Billy shouted loudly, hoping he might just wake someone else up from nearby.

The shadow loomed closer, leaning forward into a crouching position. The zip on the entrance flap began to move upwards.

'WHO IS IT?' Billy shouted again. 'IT'S NOT FUNNY!'

The zip continued upwards, moving slowly.

Billy sat up and clenched his fist. Calum sat up and shone his torch towards the entrance, desperate to see a friendly face.

'FOR THE LAST TIME . . . WHO IS IT?' Billy yelled.

The zip carried on up to the top. The flaps opened and a stooping man holding an old-fashioned lantern poked his head through. Billy and Calum screamed together and dived back into their sleeping bags.

'WHO . . . WHO ARE YOU?' Billy stammered, peeping over the edge of his sleeping bag. The light from the old lamp lit up the man's head. Greasy hair sprouted from the rim of a flat cap; the face thin and sharp with pockmarked skin . . . hollowed cheekbones and a long, twisted nose.

'Eli Knapp, if it's any business o' thee!'

Calum surfaced from his sleeping bag. The two boys stared at the hideous face. The eyes were the worst . . . dark and piercing . . . the man's expression extremely threatening.

'Wh . . . what do you want?' Billy stuttered.

The man stretched his bony arm into the tent, his lamp blinding the two boys. 'Ah want thee to keep away from things that don't concern thee!'

'What things?' Calum shouted defiantly.

'As ah said . . . from things that don't concern thee!' The man drew the lamp back, allowing the boys to see again.

With the light held closer to his face, his features looked even scarier. His thin lips were curled into a snarl, blackened and broken teeth showing through.

Billy's brain sprang into action.

OK, so the man looked scary – there was no doubt about that. But he was no seven-foot phantom Viking. As far as Billy could guess, the head belonged to some skinny scrawny bully of a man. And in any case, Dude and the other boys would surely wake up if he and Calum made enough noise.

Calum's heavy rubber torch was lying between them, and it was still lit.

Billy took a deep breath, picked it up and lunged at the face. 'WAHHHHH!' He screamed his war cry as he attacked. He struck out and landed an enormous blow . . . and hit the A-pole holding up the tent.

Billy's world turned upside down and plunged into blackness.

'GERROFF!' Calum shrieked from somewhere beside him.

Billy struggled and struggled, fighting against the canvas, desperate to get himself upright again. But the more he fought, the more he seemed to get into a tangle.

'WHAT ON EARTH'S GOING ON?' a familiar voice sounded from somewhere near.

'HELP!' Calum shrieked. 'WE'RE BEING ATTACKED!'

More voices sounded, and then Billy was aware of the tent material being lifted away. A few minutes later, which seemed like an eternity, he and Calum were dragged through the tent opening and out into the cool night air.

Mr Duder and some of the boys stood around, shining their torches into their terror-stricken faces.

'What happened?' Matthew asked, his eyes still sleepy.

'We heard you screaming.'

'A man sneaked up to our tent and poked his head in,' Calum told them.

Billy nodded. 'It's true. You should have seen his face . . . it scared the life out of us.'

'Well you're full of life again now,' Mr Duder said without smiling. 'I didn't see anyone when I came over. All I heard was you two yelling at the top of your voices.'

Oliver stood with his arms folded, 'No doubt a nightmare due to an overactive imagination. I have them all the time.'

'I think Ollie's right,' Mr Duder said. 'It's hardly surprising in view of all the earlier goings on. Though it must have been one heck of a nightmare. You pulled the tent down!'

'But . . . but . . . I saw . . .'

Calum didn't get a chance to finish. '. . . The lights,' Billy interrupted. 'Yes . . . that's what I saw. It must have been Dude's . . . I mean Mr Duder's torch. You're right, sir. Just a nightmare. Sorry, sir.'

Billy glared at Calum and Calum got the message.

'OK, lads!' Mr Duder said in a calmer voice. 'Let's get this tent back into shape so that Laurel and Hardy here can get back in their sleeping bags . . . and then maybe we can all get some sleep!'

The boys laughed and Billy and Calum pretended to laugh with them. Whilst they set about re-erecting the tent, Billy kept glancing around, looking for a distant light or any sign of their scary visitor. But there was nothing.

Fifteen minutes later the tent was back up and the two friends were gratefully slipping back into their sleeping bags.

'Thanks, sir!' Calum said meekly.

'Thanks, sir!' Billy said thoughtfully.

'OK! Now let's all try and get some sleep. We should have a quieter day tomorrow. We're going to see the old abbey. Surely nothing can go wrong there!'

The schoolteacher and the other boys retired to their tents and Billy and Calum lay awake for another hour, going over and over everything. Neither of them could make head nor tail of what had happened.

'OK, Billy! We'd better try and get some sleep. Goodnight!' Calum's head disappeared into his sleeping bag.

'Hang on a minute,' Billy said. 'When we first saw that man's head poking through . . . did he say his name?'

Calum didn't move, but a muffled reply sounded from somewhere deep within his sleeping bag, 'Eli . . . Eli Knapp.'

Billy felt an icy shiver run down his spine.

The phone call home . . . to his mum! She'd warned him about someone called Eli . . . wearing a flat cap. 'A nasty piece of work' she'd said. And the tea leaves . . . before he'd left for the camping trip . . . she'd seen someone tall, dark and unfriendly!

That was it . . . there was no doubt that the face in the tent belonged to the same creep that his mum had fore-warned him about!

Billy had no idea who Eli Knapp was, and he didn't really want to know.

But there was no doubt in his mind that whether he liked it or not, he was destined to meet up with this nasty piece of work again!

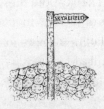

15
UNDERCOVER PLANS

Mr Duder's voice sounded from outside the tent. 'Come on, sleepyheads . . . get a move on!'

Billy groaned, yawned and rolled over. He looked at his watch . . . nine o'clock! Wow! Breakfast was at eight-thirty. It was unusual for Billy and Calum to be late – they were nearly always up and about well before they needed to be.

He dug Calum in the ribs. 'Come on! Get up . . . we're late!'

While Calum stirred, Billy sat up and thought back to last night's events. It was hardly surprising that the two of them had slept in. They'd both struggled to get back to sleep after the chaos of their chilling night-time visit.

A short while later, another voice sounded from outside. It was Sam. 'Hey! Laurel and Hardy! Dotty says if you want any breakfast, you've got ten minutes before it's all cleared away!'

'OK!' Billy shouted back. 'We're on our way.'

Calum sat up and rubbed his eyes. 'I don't really want any breakfast. I'm still stuffed from last night!'

Billy had to agree. That supper had been a *humongous* feast. It was a wonder anyone wanted any breakfast.

Five minutes later, the two of them were up and dressed, but feeling really tired. They stretched and yawned and neither of them said very much. When they finally arrived at breakfast, they found the two teachers and the Year 7s sitting around a couple of foldaway tables decked with various cereal packets, milk and fruit juices. Billy noted that there was little evidence of dirty dishes. Most of the group were sipping drinks. It seemed that everyone felt just like he and Calum did . . . full up from last night's supper!

'OK! Now that Laurel and Hardy have managed to join us . . .' Mr Duder began. '. . . I'll tell you today's plans.'

The Year 7s looked on in anticipation.

Mr Duder folded his arms and continued. 'As I said yesterday, we're driving over to an old abbey about half an hour from here. It's called Belton Priory and it has a fascinating history.'

'And no wolves!' Matthew added cheekily.

'Certainly not!' Miss Dingle chipped in. She sipped the rest of her orange juice, slipped her bag over her shoulder and moved up beside Mr Duder.

'I don't suppose there are any shops to look round,' Kelsey sighed.

'Actually . . . yes,' Mr Duder smiled. 'There's a gift shop. It'll be an opportunity to buy a few souvenirs and maybe send a postcard home.'

The mention of a gift shop seemed to cheer the girls up.

From Billy's point of view, the trip offered an opportunity to get away from the campsite and the environs of Howling Ghyll. He needed time to think . . . time to get things clear in his mind.

A battered old car passed along the road bordering the campsite. The engine coughed and spluttered and everyone looked up.

'Wow! That car sounds like a heap of junk,' Sam laughed.

'It's the exhaust!' Oliver said in his usual matter-of-fact way. 'It's blowing back. It's probably rusted through and full of holes.'

They all watched as the car slowed towards the entrance to the campsite. It pulled into the gravel car park by the side of the farmhouse and shuddered to a halt. A familiar figure clambered out.

Billy's heart began to beat faster. *It was Father Boniface!*

'It's that nice guy from yesterday,' Kelsey informed everyone.

'And it looks like he's coming over here,' Calum added.

Mr Duder turned back towards them, 'Yes . . . he's going with us to the priory. He phoned me earlier this morning. He's going to lead and we're going to follow behind. And when we get there, he's offered to give us a guided tour. Father Boniface knows the history of the priory right back to the days when it was first built . . . sometime in the 12th century, I think he said.'

'Big wow!' Kelsey Cartwright muttered loud enough for everyone to hear.

Miss Dingle gave her an icy stare.

'Sorry, miss!' Kelsey said quietly.

'Good morning!' Father Boniface shouted cheerily as he approached them.

Billy tensed as the priest looked straight at him.

'It's a grand day,' Father Boniface said, looking up at the blue sky. 'And it's just as well, because much of the old abbey is in ruins. There's little cover if it rains.'

'Well at least there's a gift shop,' Kelsey chipped in sulkily.

The priest nodded. 'Quite right, young lady! And there's also a rather nice tea room that serves the most delicious cakes and ice cream.'

Suddenly, the Year 7s perked up. Last night's supper seemed instantly forgotten.

Mr Duder brought everyone back to the present, 'OK, you guys! Chop chop! I want you all ready to go in ten minutes. We'll meet by the minibus.'

'Mr Duder!' the priest interrupted. 'May I offer to take a couple of your pupils in my car? It will give the rest of you more room to stretch out. I know how cramped minibuses can be.'

Mr Duder looked thoughtful. He glanced across at Miss Dingle. 'That's very kind of you, Father . . .'

'Well, that's settled then!' The priest said quickly. 'My old car may be a bit noisy, but Maisie . . . that's her name . . . she's as reliable and steadfast as she ever was.' He pointed over towards Billy and Calum. 'How about you two? You always seem to be together.'

Billy's heart beat even faster.

'You mean Laurel and Hardy!' Sam yelled out.

The Year 7s chuckled.

'Well . . . if you're sure . . .' Mr Duder said, still hesitating.

'It's OK with us, sir,' Billy said with as much confidence

as he could muster.

'Well that's fine then, Mr Duder,' the priest smiled.

Ten minutes later, the priest's car spluttered into action as it led the minibus out of the campsite and headed off towards Belton Priory. Billy sat in the front, alongside Father Boniface, and Calum sat in the back. At first no one spoke. The atmosphere in the old car was tense. Billy sensed that the journey to the priory would be more than interesting. The priest had wanted to talk to him and this was his chance.

A few minutes later, after climbing out of Skyrefield and heading down the hill on the other side, Father Boniface glanced sideways. 'OK, lads! I know it's a lot to ask – you hardly know me – but you have to trust me. If anything out of the ordinary has happened to either of you since you arrived here . . . would you mind telling me about it?'

Billy and Calum looked at each other. They both nodded.

Billy took a deep breath, but it was Calum who spoke first. 'I'll tell you!' he said. 'That's *my* job. Billy gets involved in all sorts of spooky goings-on and I get sucked in with him. And then I try to help him sort things out. It's how we work.'

Father Boniface smiled and nodded at the same time. 'Very well! I'm listening!'

As the priest stared forward, eyes fixed firmly on the road, Calum told him all the weird things that had happened since they'd arrived at the campsite. He told the priest about the dead animals hanging on fences, the legend of the 'Moonwailer' that Mr Duder had told them about, the weird goings-on during the visit to the mine site and finally about the spooky visit from Eli Knapp, and how Billy's mother had predicted it.

At the mention of Eli Knapp, the priest almost let go of the steering wheel. 'Good Lord in heaven!' he said. 'You saw Eli Knapp?'

'Yes,' Billy said meekly. 'He frightened us. He seemed nasty.'

'Oh, he's nasty alright,' Father Boniface said firmly. 'He's straight from the Devil!' The car slowed and the priest glanced sideways, straight into Billy's face. 'And there's something else you should know about Eli Knapp,' he said mysteriously. 'Something you're going to find hard to believe . . .'

'What's that?' Calum asked excitedly, from the back seat.

The priest looked into his driving mirror and fixed his gaze on Calum. *Eli Knapp has been dead for a very long time!*

As Billy and Calum gasped, the priest's eyes went back to the road. He drove on slowly, glancing in the wing mirror to check that the school minibus was still following behind.

'So who is he?' Billy asked.

'He's the stepfather of the twin boys . . . Jacob and Isaac . . . in the story that your teacher told you. Only it's not just a story. It's true!'

Billy and Calum looked at each other in amazement.

Father Boniface continued in a solemn tone of voice. 'One night, the mining community got together. They decided to bring Eli Knapp to justice and rescue the surviving twin, Isaac, from his evil clutches.'

'But when they got there, the miner and the boy had disappeared,' Calum chipped in. 'Mr Duder told us.'

The priest stared ahead and nodded. 'It seems that Eli got wind they were coming and decided to do something about it.'

'How do you mean?' Billy asked, suspecting the worst.

'He dragged the poor boy out on to the moor and shot him, then buried him in a shallow grave.'

'That's evil!' Calum groaned from the backseat.

'So what happened to the miner,' Billy asked.

'Disappeared! Never seen again. It's said that he fled to the coast and took up somewhere abroad.'

'So he got away with it!' Billy sighed.

'Not quite . . .' Father Boniface answered mysteriously. 'There's a story amongst the locals that later on that fateful night, the boy dug himself out of his grave.'

'So he wasn't dead?' Billy and Calum asked together.

The priest shook his head. 'Mortally wounded . . . but not dead! He crawled, dying, over the moor towards the standing stone, desperate to reach his brother's grave.'

Billy swallowed hard, 'Did he make it?'

'Yes . . . but only with the Devil's help! Such was the boy's hatred for his stepfather and his determination to reach Jacob's grave, he foolishly made a deal with Satan.'

Calum leaned forward from the backseat. 'What was the deal?'

'Immortality! A chance to live on and exact his revenge on his evil stepfather.'

'But what did the Devil get out of it?' Calum asked.

'Well . . . the legend says that the boy was only allowed to live on in the form of a werewolf . . . a true creature of Satan!'

'Wow!' Billy gasped, looking at Calum.

'But how can the werewolf . . . I mean the Moonwailer

. . . ever get revenge?' Calum asked, his eyes wider than ever. 'Like you said, Eli Knapp's been dead for a long time.'

Father Boniface sighed. 'The poor beast doesn't know that. He'll play out his Moonwailer role forever . . . *unless* . . . someone can put a stop to it.'

Billy gulped. He sensed he was about to find out exactly what Father Boniface had in mind for him.

The priest glanced sideways, 'You have the gift, Billy!'

'What do you mean?'

'Eli Knapp and the Moonwailer are not the only demons you've encountered, are they? I overheard you talking to Calum in the drying room. It seems you've been involved with other restless spirits.'

'But I don't try to!' Billy said solemnly.

The priest smiled, 'As I said back at the hall, "The Lord works in mysterious ways!".'

Billy didn't really understand. He nodded his head and looked through the windscreen at the rolling hills and green fields . . . a beautiful landscape as far as the eye could see. It was difficult to believe that any evil could exist in a place like this.

'We'll soon be at the priory,' Father Boniface informed them.

'And now let me tell you something about me. As we're in this together, I think you've a right to know.'

Brilliant! Billy thought to himself. There was so much he wanted to know about Father Boniface, but he felt uncomfortable questioning a grown up.

'I came here, to Percival Hall, three years ago,' the priest began. 'I'd been working too hard in my parish, so I came hear for a little bit of "R and R".'

Billy looked puzzled.

Father Boniface smiled. 'Rest and Relaxation! I intended to stay for six months.'

'So why did you stay on?' Calum asked.

The priest stared through the windscreen. 'It wasn't long before I heard about the Moonwailer. The others staying at the hall chatted about it. The landlord of the local inn told me the history of it. To tourists it was just local superstition . . . a creepy story to tell children at bedtime . . . nothing more. But I became curious and began researching the legend, looking into church records, talking to the older villagers. I suppose you could say that I became obsessed by the whole thing.'

'So is that why you stayed on?' Calum suggested. '. . . To solve the mystery?'

The priest nodded. 'You could say that . . . but after being awoken one night . . . my curiosity got the better of me.'

'You went out!' Calum said, his voice shaking with anticipation.

Father Boniface nodded again. 'I went out under a crescent moon. I know now that was a foolish thing to do. And you know what happened to me!' he said, raising his hooked hand.

'So you weren't really medicating?' Billy asked, his eyes wide.

'You mean *meditating*, Billy . . . and no, I wasn't. I was out hunting . . . for the Moonwailer. I'm still not sure how I survived to tell the tale. I was found unconscious. I woke up in Skipdale hospital.'

'Did you tell them what happened?' Calum asked.

'Oh, I told them. I ranted and raved and tried to tell

them about the Moonwailer creature . . . but they would have none of it. They said I was suffering from shock and my senses were all over the place.'

'Delirious!' Calum suggested.

'Exactly! The authorities even ridiculed me . . . said I was mentally unbalanced . . . said it was probably why I was staying at the hall in the first place!'

'That's horrible!' Billy sighed.

'I finally began to doubt myself. As I recovered from my injuries, I began to tell people what they wanted to believe – that a wild animal had attacked me. The police said I was right – they came up with the Canadian timberwolf story. In the end I agreed with them.'

'Why?' Billy and Calum asked together.

The priest smiled to himself. 'Because it took the heat off me, as they say in the movies. As soon as I was stronger, I started my research again. I promised myself that one day I would help the Moonwailer find justice . . . remove its curse and send it back to its resting place . . . make the area safe again . . . my good deed for humanity. I even convinced myself that I'd been chosen by God . . . like it was my mission.'

The car slowed again, and took a sharp bend. Billy saw the sign by the edge of the road – BELTON PRIORY – 1 MILE.

'But I was never able to fulfil my mission,' the priest continued. 'Something was missing . . . and I didn't know what it was.'

'So do you know now?' Calum asked.

The priest took his eyes momentarily off the road and glanced at Billy again. 'Yes! I believe that Billy was brought here. He's the missing piece of the puzzle.'

'How . . . how do you mean?' Billy's voice trembled.

The priest looked through the windscreen again. 'The Moonwailer is haunting the ghyll with two things in mind.'

'Ww . . . what are they?' Billy asked nervously..

'To guard his brother's grave . . . up by the Devil's Tooth . . . and to avenge his brother's death . . . face up to his evil stepfather . . . destroy him. Only then will the creature depart this earthly plane.'

Billy stared ahead with his mouth open, 'So where do I come in?'

'It is our job, Billy – you and I – to bring these two spirits together. I can find the Moonwailer . . . however, as a priest, I'm not in the business of raising spirits. But you can! You have the power to bring Eli Knapp to us. You've done it once already, and you can do it again!'

Calum leaned forward and poked his head between Billy and the priest. 'And how are you both going to do that . . . and when?'

The priest hesitated, 'I'm still working out the "how" bit, but we need to act tonight. The Moonwailer favours the crescent moon. Tonight it is in its final phase and the creature will be on the prowl. If we miss this opportunity we'll have to wait another month . . . and you'll be back at home.'

A road sign loomed in front, informing them that the priory was just around the next bend.

'We'll meet by the entrance to the campsite at eleven thirty tonight,' the priest continued. 'Keep out of sight . . . I'll do the same. And whatever you do . . . tell no one.'

'Am I included in all of this,' Calum asked nervously.

Father Boniface looked at him hard through his driving mirror. 'It's up to you!'

'Well count me in,' Calum said sternly. 'Where Billy goes, I go. It's like I said . . . we're a team.'

The ruins of Belton Priory appeared in a field over to their left. 'That's settled then,' Father Boniface said. 'Eleven thirty tonight. Leave the rest to me.'

The car slowed and turned into a car park. The school minibus drew up behind.

'One last thing,' Billy said anxiously. 'How dangerous do you think it's going to be for us with the Moonwailer lurking out there?'

The priest parked the old car, pulled on the handbrake and switched off the engine. He turned to face Billy, lifted his metal hook and pointed to the scar under his eye.

'Do you really need to ask, Billy? We can only trust in the grace of God.'

Billy nodded solemnly. Calum did the same.

The priest had left them in no doubt. *It was a very dangerous mission!*

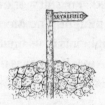

16
FRIGHT
NIGHT

The day out turned out to be more entertaining than anyone would have guessed.

Father Boniface had amused everyone guiding them around the old abbey. During his tour he'd described the harsh way of life that the Augustinian monks had endured over the years. He'd told how Belton Priory had been involved in ancient battles. He'd even told of an unfortunate monk walled up alive and left to die.

'On certain nights you can still hear his screams,' Mr Duder had added in a spooky voice.

The day had been rounded off with a visit to the gift shop and on at last to the tea room. The cakes and ice cream had been delicious – the Year 7s agreed they'd been well worth waiting for!

At the end of the visit Sam and Matthew had asked if

they could travel back in Father Boniface's car. The priest had agreed. Billy realised that he'd had no choice – if he'd requested the company of himself and Calum again, it might have raised suspicion.

So Billy and Calum sat next to each other in the school minibus as it headed back towards Skyrefield. The other Year 7s chatted excitedly about their day. Billy and Calum remained quiet, both thinking ahead to their meeting with Father Boniface, nervous of what the night might hold in store for them.

When they finally arrived back at the campsite, Billy saw a familiar small boy standing by the gate with a familiar dog.

'Look! It's Elvis!' Billy exclaimed.

'And Quicksilver!' Calum added.

As they clambered out of the minibus, Billy saw that Matthew and Sam had already got out of the priest's car and ran over to them. Matthew was saying something to Elvis and Sam was stroking the dog's head affectionately.

Father Boniface approached Mr Duder and spoke quietly to him.

'OK!' Mr Duder shouted when they were all off the bus. 'Father Boniface has to go now. I think we all need to say something!'

Kelsey looked blank.

'Thank you!' Martine said, giving her a nudge.

'Oops! Thank you!' Kelsey said, smiling coyly.

The other Year 7s laughed and joined in a chorus of 'thank you'.

The priest glanced at Billy and gave him a knowing look. 'Have a good evening,' he said loudly, still fixing his eyes on Billy. 'I'd love to stay a bit longer, but I've got some work to do back at the hall.'

A few minutes later Father Boniface drove away up the lane and Mr Duder turned to the Year 7s. 'Miss Dingle and I are going to make a cup of tea. You lot can chill out for a bit. There's a bat and ball in the boot of the minibus if anyone feels like running off a bit of energy.'

The girls didn't look too enthusiastic. They slouched off in the direction of their tents without looking back. Oliver walked away in a similar manner.

Billy and Calum went over to Elvis. 'Hi!' Billy said. 'What are you up to?'

'He's been rabbiting!' Sam answered for him.

'That's right!' Elvis said, with a big grin on his freckled face. 'We caught three. I snared two of 'em, and Quicksilver caught the other.' He patted the greyhound proudly on the head. The dog looked up at him and panted enthusiastically.

'Well . . . where are they?' Calum asked, his voice full of surprise.

'Where's what?' Elvis grinned.

'The rabbits.'

'Oh . . . they were old. No good to eat. So we hung them round the edge of our field. We put them on fences . . . to keep the old 'uns happy. They think that dead rabbits keep bad things away.'

Billy looked at Calum, and then to Elvis. 'What do you mean by "bad things"?'

'Well . . . evil spirits and stuff! That's why we always camp by the beck – the old 'uns say that we're safe as long as we've got water by us – even the beast won't cross it.'

'The Moonwailer!' Billy and Calum said together.

Elvis looked up at them with wide eyes. 'So you've

heard of it? My dad and his mates think it's just a dog . . . a stray gone wild. It's been killing sheep, see . . . and the police have been around.'

'Yes . . . we know . . . but your dad and his mates are wrong. It's no wild dog!' Calum informed him.

Billy nodded. 'We've seen it . . . up in Howling Ghyll.'

Elvis gawped at them. 'Wow! I've been up there this afternoon. I set a load of fresh snares.'

'Well don't go back,' Calum said sternly.

'Naw . . . I'm not scared!' Elvis replied. He looked down at Quicksilver and patted his head. ' In any case, I've got Quicksilver. He can be as fierce as a wild bear when he wants to.'

'He'd need to be.' Billy told him. 'Anyway . . . can I just ask you . . . would you kill a fox and hang it on a fence?'

Elvis shook his head. 'No way! Dad says we should respect foxes. They do more good than 'arm.'

'What are you thinking, Billy?' Calum asked.

'The fox on the campsite fence – I think the Moonwailer put it there – to mark his territory!'

'And the log fence up at Howling Ghyll,' Calum went on, 'the dead sheep!'

Elvis looked at them open-mouthed. 'Well it wasn't us. We only use rabbits and we only put them around our field.'

Billy looked thoughtful. But then a shout from some-where behind caused them all to turn round. A few of the Year 7 boys had started a game with a bat and ball. Someone had hit the ball high into the air and it was drop-ping just over to their left.

Without hesitation, Quicksilver turned and sprinted off. As the ball plummeted to the ground, the dog leapt high into the air and caught it cleanly in its mouth.

'Wow!' Billy and Calum gasped together. The other Year 7 boys rushed over and began fussing the dog.

Elvis gave a sharp whistle. Quicksilver dropped the ball and sprinted back to his side.

'That is some dog!' Calum said admiringly.

'Well . . . got to go!' Elvis said, a big grin on his face.

'OK! See ya!' Calum said.

'Don't forget! Keep away from Howling Ghyll!' Billy shouted after him.

Elvis looked back and smiled. And then he and the dog sprinted off.

'If that thing we saw *was* the Moonwailer, do you think Quicksilver would really stand a chance against it?' Calum said thoughtfully.

Billy turned and looked out across the fields towards the limestone hills. 'It *was* the Moonwailer . . . you can be sure of that. And as for Elvis's dog . . . it wouldn't stand a chance.'

Calum nodded. 'Shall we join in with the others?' he asked, looking in the direction of the ball game.

'No . . . I'm not really in the mood,' Billy said quietly. 'My mind wouldn't be on it.'

Calum nodded again. 'You're right! Let's go over to Dude and Dotty and grab a cup of tea.'

Despite everything, Billy started laughing. "Dude and Dotty" sounded like some sort of comedy double act. 'OK!' Billy agreed, still chuckling. 'Let's ask Dude and Dotty!'

*

After another hearty supper – this time burgers followed

by steamed treacle sponge and custard – everyone headed back to their tents to settle down for the night. Billy and Calum zipped themselves in and talked on endlessly.

Some time later, Billy checked his watch – 9.45 – still well over an hour to go.

It was about ten o'clock when Mr Duder appeared on his usual round. 'Goodnight, boys,' he said quietly from outside the tent.

'Goodnight, sir,' they both replied, trying to sound sleepy.

As the time neared eleven thirty, the two friends put a few things into their backpacks and readied themselves for the off. Calum suggested that they stuff some loose clothes into their sleeping bags to make it look as if they were still tucked up inside. There was always the possibility that Dude might check them again during the night.

Billy shone Calum's torch onto his watch – 11.26. 'Come on! Let's go.'

Calum reached into one of the side pockets stitched into the side of the tent and took out a plastic wallet.

'What's that?' Billy asked,

Calum opened the wallet and Billy shone the torch onto it. It was a small case divided into two halves. In the lower section there was a pair of tweezers, a nail file, a small pocket knife and various other bits and pieces. The top half held a small rectangular mirror.

'Looks a bit girly!' Billy teased.

Calum snapped it shut and shoved it into his rucksack. 'You never know when some of those things might come in handy,' he replied defensively.

The two boys slipped quietly out through the tent flaps. Everyone seemed to be asleep. No lights showed from any of the tents.

The night was cool and clear. Billy looked up at the sky – it was dotted with stars. In the distance above the dark outline of hills . . . the crescent moon hung in all its splendour. The sight of it sent a shiver down Billy's spine.

'Look!' Calum said, breaking the spell. 'I think I can see Father Boniface over by the gate. He's waving at us.'

Billy strained his eyes towards the campsite entrance. Calum was right. Even in the shadows Billy recognised the solid figure of the priest. He seemed to be holding something over his arm. They crouched low and crept over to the gate.

'Good lads! This way!' the familiar voice of Father Boniface called quietly to them.

As Billy and Calum approached, they both gasped. The priest was carrying a rifle. It was a double barrel shotgun and it was breached across his metal arm.

'Ah . . . the gun!' the priest said, seeing the surprised look on the boys' faces.

'Are you going to try and shoot the Moonwailer?' Billy asked.

'All will be explained,' Father Boniface answered. He was wearing a tight woolly cap and had a small rucksack on his back. With his cap, backpack and gun, and his face in shadow, he gave Billy the impression of a commando on a night mission.

'Well . . . where are we going?' Calum asked.

'Away up the footpath, heading towards the old mining site – the one you visited with your school party. We're going to stop off somewhere on the way, and then we'll head off to the Devil's Tooth.'

Billy and Calum turned to face each other. Even in

shadow, Billy could guess the expression on Calum's face. They both knew exactly what each other was thinking.

'And . . . and . . . that's where the Moonwailer will be!' Calum stammered.'

The priest turned towards them. It was too dark to see his eyes, but his hooked hand stood out clearly in the half-light.

'Exactly! That's why we're heading there,' the priest said solemnly, '. . . *and we're going to take the spirit of Eli Knapp with us!*'

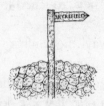

17
MISSION IMPOSSIBLE

Three shadowy figures made their way alongside Howling Beck, heading north towards the old mine workings. Father Boniface led the way, the shotgun breached over his metal wrist, his one good hand at the ready.

The stars twinkled above their heads, the crescent moon standing out in the distance. The stream bubbled and gurgled by their side.

'Is is right that the Moonwailer won't cross water?' Billy whispered to the priest.

Father Boniface turned his head. 'Yes . . . how did you know that?'

'A boy told us. He lives on the camp in one of the caravans.'

'One of the travellers no doubt,' the priest said in a low voice. 'The story of the Moonwailer is not unknown to them . . . especially to some of the older ones.'

'Why water?' Calum asked.

'Water is a mirror . . . it reflects the truth. The travellers are right! We should keep the stream as close to us as we can for as long as we can.'

Billy listened to the water gurgling beside them. His mind went back to that first night at the campsite . . . filling the water carrier . . . staring at his reflection in the stream . . . the horrific howling . . . falling into the freezing water!

He was just about to ask another question when the priest picked up the pace a little. A few minutes later Billy saw the outline of the ruined barn.

Calum pointed to it. 'That's where Sam jumped out.'

'I know,' Billy replied, wishing that it was daylight and that they were with the other Year 7s again. He envied them snug in their tents, not having a clue what he and Calum were up to.

As they approached the derelict barn, the priest stopped abruptly and held them back. 'Billy! Do you feel anything?'

Billy concentrated. 'No! Nothing!'

'There's something up ahead . . . I'm sure of it,' the priest whispered. 'Pass me the torch.'

Calum was carrying his large rubber torch. Father Boniface had said to use it only in an emergency. If they used the torch to light the way, they would be spotted too easily.

Calum handed it over. The priest switched it on and aimed its powerful beam along the footpath towards the building. Something stirred ahead . . . they all heard it.

'Here . . . you take the torch,' Father Boniface instructed Calum. 'I'll ready the gun.'

As the priest snapped the gun shut and aimed it forward, Calum moved up beside him and illuminated the footpath. The three of them crept on a few more paces. Billy felt his heart begin to race. Something was definitely moving about amongst a dense patch of ferns growing alongside the building.

A few steps closer and they heard a loud rustling.

The priest stopped and aimed his gun. 'COME OUT!' He yelled so loudly that Calum almost dropped his torch.

In the same instant a snarling animal leapt towards them, its eyes blazing in the torchlight and fangs bared at the ready. Instead of firing the gun, the priest jumped to one side. Calum shrieked and dropped the torch. Billy grabbed the startled animal by the neck and tried to calm it.

'*Quicksilver!* It's OK . . . it's me . . . Elvis's friend.'

The dog yelped and licked Billy's face.

Calum picked up the torch just in time to see Elvis appear from behind the barn. 'Thank God it's you. You scared me to death!'

'We frightened *you*!' Billy said, still stroking Quicksilver. 'Your dog almost gave us a heart attack.'

'And almost got shot!' Father Boniface said, breaching his gun again. I only just managed to stop myself. You must be the traveller that Billy mentioned earlier. I can't believe you would be out here on your own. What would your parents think?'

Elvis looked at the priest with a sheepish expression. 'I've only got my dad, and he's out here with me. He's just over the other side of the beck checking a couple of rabbit snares. I'm waiting for him.'

'He obviously doesn't know how dangerous it is out here,' the priest frowned.

'His dad doesn't believe in the Moonwailer; he just thinks it's a wild dog,' Billy said.

Elvis nodded.

Before anyone else had chance to speak, a blood-curdling howl filled their ears. It came from somewhere up at the head of the narrow valley and it echoed through the cool night air.

Quicksilver whined.

Everyone else seemed frozen . . . unable to speak.

It was Elvis who broke the silence. 'I'm scared. I want my dad.'

'Come on. Show us where these traps were set,' Father Boniface said reassuringly. 'We'll find him.'

'Quicksilver will take us to him . . . won't you boy.' Elvis said. He fastened a leash to the dog's collar. 'Come on, boy! Where's Dad?'

The dog seemed to understand. It lurched forward and pulled Elvis down the grassy slope towards the stream. With the aid of the torch they all managed to scramble across the beck and on towards the foot of a large hill on the other side. A forest of ferns sprouted up in front of them and they ploughed through it following Quicksilver's course up the side of the hill.

It wasn't long before they heard a groaning moaning sound from somewhere in front.

'Dad . . . is that you?' Elvis called as loudly as he dare.

Quicksilver ploughed on another few metres, and then they found him . . . lying on the ground . . . covered in blood.

Elvis dropped to his knees. The dog began licking the injured man's face.

'Don't crowd him,' Father Boniface instructed, as Calum shone the torch over the man's broken body. 'He's badly hurt. Give him space.'

Billy swallowed hard as he saw the damage to Elvis's dad. His head was covered in blood . . . and some of his right ear was missing.

'Get me away from here!' the man moaned.

Father Boniface knelt by his side. 'We're going to get you over to the other side of the beck. We'll put you in the old barn. You'll be safe there till the ambulance arrives.'

It was only a short distance, but Elvis's father was a heavy man and was unable to walk. With the boys' help, the priest somehow managed to get the crumpled body onto his broad shoulders. Calum carried the breached shotgun whilst Father Boniface stepped forward, carrying the injured man in 'fireman's lift' style.

Once inside the barn they laid him as comfortably as they could on a pile of musty old straw. The priest dialled 999 on his mobile, told them exactly where they were situated and requested an ambulance. He took the rucksack of his back, rummaged around in it and took out a small first-aid kit. A short while later he was kneeling at the man's side, attending to his wounds.

'Dad . . . what happened?' Elvis said, tears trickling down his cheeks.

'Something came at me from behind. I didn't stand a chance!'

Father Boniface wiped the blood from the victim's face and tried to dress his damaged ear. But he couldn't rid the poor man of his expression of terror. Billy had never seen anyone look so frightened.

'Did you get a look at it?' Calum asked.

The man winced with pain. 'No . . . it was all a blur . . . too much blood . . . *my blood*! I can't believe it . . . but all those stories about the beast . . . *I think they're true!'*

'That's why we're here,' the priest said softly to him, 'to free these hills from the Moonwailer. Lucky for you we came along.'

Elvis's dad groaned. He reached down to his ankle. His trouser leg had been ripped away and a row of teeth marks stood out in the torn flesh of his shin.

'Believe me,' he moaned, 'you don't stand a chance. The Moonwailer . . . or whatever you call it . . . *it's straight from Hell!'*

'Fortunately, we have God on our side,' Father Boniface replied.

'You're not taking the boys with you . . . surely?'

'We'll leave Elvis here with you to look out for the ambulance. He'll need to guide the paramedics up here.'

The man slumped back on his bed of straw. He looked about to faint. 'Well . . . take the dog . . .' he gasped. 'He'll be the first to know if the beast's about. Take him with you!'

'But Dad . . .'Elvis protested.

'Stop worrying, son! That beast is fast . . . but nothing on earth can catch Quicksilver.'

Elvis stopped protesting and handed the dog's leash over. Billy took it reluctantly and looked thoughtful.

Like Elvis's dad had said, nothing on earth could catch Quicksilver, but Billy knew enough about the Moonwailer to know . . . that the beast really was . . . *like nothing on earth!*

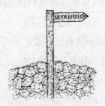

18
SIXTH SENSE

Billy, Calum and the priest resumed their path alongside the beck, heading onwards under a starlit sky. Billy led at the front, Quicksilver straining at his leash and pulling him on. After a little while the footpath left the beck, skirted the edge of a hill and began to climb. The sound of running water far below made Billy feel more vulnerable . . . he preferred the 'water barrier' to be close at hand. Judging by Calum's sideways glance, he felt the same.

'OK!' Father Boniface said from behind. 'Stop and let me take the front . . . we need to leave the main path for a while.'

The priest led them up a steeper path . . . straight up the hillside . . . cutting through a forest of ferns. The going was tough and they all breathed heavily. Quicksilver panted and continued to pull at his leash. As they worked around a high ridge, Billy saw the distant ruins of another small building silhouetted against the night sky.

'Keep going!' Father Boniface urged them over his shoulder. 'We're almost there!'

The dark ruins of the dilapidated building loomed closer.

'Is that where we're heading?' Calum asked.

'Yes!' the priest replied, without looking back.

A short while later they walked up to the crumbling shell of an old cottage. The roof had completely gone, but the doorway was still there and a few of the window spaces survived within the old stonework.

Calum was the first to spot the rusted iron framework by the side of the doorway. 'What's that?'

Father Boniface stood by Calum's side. 'Can't you guess?'

'I can!' Billy said, as Quicksilver towed him up beside them. 'It's where the pit bull terriers were kept.'

'Oh my God!' Calum said. 'This was Eli Knapp's cottage.'

The priest turned towards him. 'You're wrong to take the good Lord's name in vain, young Calum, but otherwise, you're right – this is where the evil man lived.'

'So why are we here?' Billy asked in a shaky voice.

Calum knelt down and stroked Quicksilver's sleek head. The dog gave a little whine. 'You're nervous, boy, aren't you?'

'And so he should be,' the priest said in a serious tone of voice. 'This place still reeks of evil. He can sense it . . . and so shall we shortly . . . once we're in there.'

Billy glanced through one of the window spaces – it looked black!

Calum walked up to the doorway, switched his torch on and aimed it inside. Something scurried across the stone-flagged floor, desperate to get out of the torchlight. 'A rat! Gross!' he uttered.

Billy pulled Quicksilver towards the doorway, determined to let him in first . . . to sniff out the rodent. But the greyhound pulled back.

'He won't go in!' Billy sighed.

'Leave him be! Tie him up outside,' Father Boniface instructed. He took the torch from Calum. 'Then follow me!'

As Billy tied the reluctant greyhound to the rusted iron framework, the priest aimed the torch into the shadows and moved inside. Billy and Calum followed close by his shoulder, watching the progress of the torch beam as it scanned around the crumbling shell.

A fireplace still existed on the left-hand wall. Father Boniface walked over to it, rummaged around in his bag and took out a candle and a box of matches. He lit the candle and stuck it on the stone shelf above the fireplace. The flickering yellow flame lit the room and revealed its dingy state.

Billy looked at the floor – everywhere, weeds and grass sprouted from the gaps between the stone floor slabs. The crumbling walls were covered in moss and lichen and were damp and musty. The roof had almost gone; just a few of the old wooden timbers, twisted and rotted, still stretching across the ceiling space.

As Billy scanned around the eerie space, no one spoke

– it seemed that Calum and the priest felt just like he did – overcome by the depressing gloom.

'Can you sense anyone's presence here, Billy?' the priest asked, breaking the tense silence.

Billy stood still and concentrated. 'Yes . . . I've got a really bad feeling.'

Calum looked at him with a worried frown.

Father Boniface switched off his torch, went over to the fireplace and took hold of the candle. He walked back and stood opposite Billy. With Calum standing by them, the trio formed a tight triangle, the priest holding the candle at the centre, lighting up their faces.

The priest looked straight at Billy. 'We need Eli Knapp,' he said determinedly. 'Only you can bring him here!'

Billy felt the panic well up inside. Calum looked at him with wide eyes. In the pale candlelight, Calum looked spooky. He reminded Billy of a zombie.

'But . . . but . . . how can I?' Billy stammered.

'Just *think* of him,' Father Boniface replied. 'That night he appeared in your tent. You saw his face. Try to remember what he looked like. Try to picture him in your mind.'

That's easy! Billy thought to himself. *How can anyone forget a face like that!*

He closed his eyes and cringed inwardly at the image of Eli Knapp's evil twisted features as they sprung up in his memory. Goosebumps spread across his body. The bad feeling was growing stronger.

'Are you OK?' Calum whispered by his side.

'I'm scared,' Billy whispered back. 'It's that face . . . I can see it really clear.'

'Keep concentrating!' Father Boniface urged. 'Keep

focusing on that face.'

All went still. The candle flickered. Three shadows wavered on the walls. All around them was silence. Nothing stirred.

Billy kept on concentrating . . . recollecting Eli Knapp's grotesque face in horrible detail . . . piercing eyes, pointed nose, snarling twisted mouth. His nerves were at breaking point now. He wanted to run . . . get away from it. He opened his eyes and looked across at Father Boniface's candlelit features . . . his steely blue eyes urging him on . . . full of hope.

And then an owl hooted from somewhere above his head and he lost his concentration. The miner's evil face disappeared from his mind. But the bad feeling was still there. Butterflies fluttered in his stomach more than before.

Billy thought he'd failed!

But when he looked at Father Boniface, he saw the priest's expression changing . . . the mouth sagging, the eyes growing wider!

Billy looked rapidly to Calum. His expression had changed too . . . he looked awestruck!

It was only then that Billy's eyes went over to the crumbling candlelit walls.

Straight in front, beyond Father Boniface, he saw the priest's stout shadow. To his left, over Calum's shoulder, he saw his friend's shadow.

So who did the shadow belong to on the right . . . the tall, stooping shadow? It didn't look like his . . . and in any case, his own shadow must be behind him.

Billy gulped and swallowed hard as he realised the

awful truth . . . there were now FOUR shadows on the walls of the creepy crumbling cottage!

19
WORST NIGHTMARES

As the three of them stared at the sinister shadow, the evil form of Eli Knapp materialized. It came straight out of the wall, waving a walking stick, and stopping a short distance in front of them. The priest switched on the torch and aimed it at the apparition.

The sharp pointed face looked straight at Billy. The dark, piercing eyes appeared even more menacing in the torchlight. *'I've already warned thee to stay away, lad!'*

'Keep back!' Father Boniface commanded. 'He's with me! They're both with me!'

The evil face sneered and took a step closer. Quicksilver growled from the doorway. The ghostly figure raised the walking stick held in its left hand. *'Ah've a good mind to smash all o' your skulls. Tha's no business being 'ere . . . interfering busybodies!'*

Billy noticed a shimmering glow surrounding Eli Knapp's ghostly form. It was the same thing he'd seen around the Bonebreaker.

'We've every right to be here,' Father Boniface said defensively. 'And in any case . . . we've come to help you.'

The phantom lowered its stick and spat onto the ground. *'How can tha possibly help me?'*

'If you lead us to the Moonwailer, I'll shoot him dead and you can go back to wherever you've come from.'

A pair of shifty eyes scanned the rifle that hung over the priest's metal arm.

The phantom raised his head, looked to the stars through the open roof and laughed a demonic laugh that sent shivers down all their spines. *'Tha thinks tha can slay that beast boy with yon firearm?'*

. Father Boniface reached into his pocket, took out a small object and held it in his outstretched palm. 'I can with this!'

The shimmering figure moved closer and peered at it.

Billy and Calum stepped back.

'Silver?'

The priest nodded. 'Correct!'

'God's own spear,' the phantom sneered. ''Tis the only thing on this fowl earth that will kill the beast. Even then . . . it would 'ave to strike the boy's heart true.'

'Correct again,' Father Boniface said, standing his ground. 'I've only got three of these silver bullets. But believe me . . . I'm a good shot!'

The phantom laughed hysterically again. *'Tha'r nowt but an old man. Does tha think beast's going to sit there while tha takes aim?'*

'That's where you come in,' the priest replied, his voice

starting to sound steadier. 'We both know that the beast . . . the Moonwailer . . . is really after you. And if you can distract it . . . I'll shoot it dead!'

'And why would tha do that for me, Churchman?'

Billy took a deep breath and spoke up. 'So that both of you can go back to where you belong . . . and this place will be safe again.'

'Well said, Billy!' the priest whispered.

The phantom turned and stared hard at the two boys.

Billy's heart began to race as the phantom's piercing stare penetrated deep within him. He could feel the evil behind those eyes. At the same time he knew that he was sending out an equal feeling of positive strength.

'Ah knew tha was coming. Ah could feel it in these auld bones o' mine.' The shimmering phantom raised his stick and pointed it upwards. *'We'd best be off. Whilst moon is small . . . beast will call.'*

With perfect timing a spine-chilling howl filled their ears. The greyhound whined. Billy, Calum and the priest stared up through the roof. The crescent moon hung brightly in the blue-black sky.

Eli Knapp looked at them and scowled. *'What tha waiting for? Tha'd better follow me!'*

They followed the evil form outside, untied Quicksilver and set off in what Billy guessed must have been the strangest procession ever seen – a shimmering phantom leading the way, a priest with a shotgun slung over his metal arm close behind, Billy himself, dragging along a reluctant greyhound and his best friend Calum wavering at the rear.

But if Billy forced a little smile to himself . . . it quickly vanished. He felt certain, that very soon, they would stumble upon the terrifying Moonwailer . . . *and there was no doubt in his mind that it would fall to Billy Hardacre to destroy it!*

*

The strange procession reached the mining site.

As they moved through the old workings the phantom waved his stick all around and uttered incomprehensible curses. Billy, Calum and the priest dropped further back, no one trusting Eli Knapp's ghostly form. Quicksilver pulled at his leash, but backwards . . . not forwards.

They rounded the far side of Black Hill and left the old mining site through a rotted five-bar gate. The phantom stopped and glared at them.

'The Standing Stone's round yon corner. Tha'll find 'im there . . . guarding his brother's grave. Ah'm staying 'ere!'

'Fine!' Father Boniface said, looking anxiously ahead. 'Leave it to us.' He snapped the gun shut and beckoned Billy and Calum to keep close.

With the phantom staying put, Quicksilver pulled to the front again. They crept over to the foot of Black Hill and edged around it towards the tall stone.

'Look! The Devil's Tooth!' Calum said nervously.

Crouching low and holding onto the dog, Billy stared forward. The stone was about two hundred metres away. It stood out clearly, silhouetted sharply against the starry sky.

'There's no sign of the Moonwailer,' Father Boniface whispered.

The greyhound gave a little whine and pulled on its lead. 'No . . . but he's close,' Billy said, trying to sound calm. 'Quicksilver can sense it . . . and so can I.'

Calum glanced at Billy with a frightened wide-eyed expression. 'So what's the plan?'

Father Boniface spoke up, 'When the creature appears, one of us will have to act as bait and lead him straight round the corner . . .'

'. . . To Eli Knapp!' Calum exclaimed. 'I get the idea . . . but who . . .'

'*Me!*' Billy said, before Calum had chance to finish his question. 'I'll do it!'

Quicksilver suddenly yelped and jerked at his lead. He caught Billy by surprise and broke free. They watched in horror as the greyhound sprinted across the grassy clearing and over to the foot of the tall stone. He sniffed around with his nose clamped to the ground.

'QUICKSILVER . . . HERE BOY!' Billy shouted as loud as he dare.

The dog ignored him . . . sniffed around a bit more . . . even cocked his leg up against the base of the stone.

'OVER HERE, BOY!' Father Boniface called out.

'It's too late!' Billy whispered. 'He's coming . . . the Moonwailer . . . he's really close.'

Billy was right. They watched in horror as Quicksilver stood erect. His ears went back and he began to snarl . . . backing away at the same time.

Billy's heart turned to ice as a sinister black shape appeared on the edge of the clearing. The shadowy form crept stealthily over towards the stone, Quicksilver still snarling and backing away. They watched in awe as the creature climbed nimbly up the side of the stone and crouched on its pinnacle. It angled its head back towards the crescent moon.

Now they could see the outline of the beast-boy clearly

. . . long sinewy arms reaching down to the rock to balance itself . . . crouching on powerful thighs edged with thick hair. The back was arched forward so that the creature rested on all fours, a mane of thick hair running down its spine. And then the head! Even from the distance, they saw the outline of the pointed ears. Its face was in shadow . . . but it was easy to imagine the fangs lining the mouth as it opened and screamed up at the moon. *Another long, chilling howl!*

Quicksilver reacted by charging forward, barking aggressively. All in an instant, the Moonwailer leapt down to the ground and faced the canine intruder.

One look at the beast was enough for the greyhound. It turned and sped off like a bat out of hell, heading straight down the south-facing footpath into Howling Ghyll. The Moonwailer charged after him and both Billy and Calum gasped at the speed of the creature.

'Now what?' Calum whispered.

'Ssshhh!' the priest said.

They crouched there, listening. All went spookily quiet. Father Boniface stood up and beckoned the boys to follow. The three of them crept over to the stone where Quicksilver had been scratching around. They crouched down again.

'We'll just have to wait,' Father Boniface said solemnly.

As the three of them waited and listened in the shadow of the stone, a horrible yelping reached their ears.

'*Quicksilver!*' Billy gasped.

The priest put his arm around Billy's shoulder. 'The dog's only hope was to get to the running water at the bottom of the ghyll, where the beck starts to flow.'

'I don't think he made it,' Calum said sadly.

'I'll say a prayer for him, but we'd better get back into hiding before the beast returns,' Father Boniface urged them. 'Let's get back to the foot of the hill. We'll be safer in the shadows over there.'

But as they turned, a shimmering figure charged towards them.

'WHY DIDN'T THA SHOOT IM? THA'R NOWT BUT USELESS!' Eli Knapp screamed at them. *'Ah'll split all o' thi skulls and leave thee for beast t' devour. At least it'll keep is mind off me for a while!'*

The phantom raised his stick and charged towards them.

'RUN!' Calum shrieked.

Father Boniface grabbed Calum's arm and held him. 'NO! YOU AND BILLY GET BEHIND ME! I'LL DEAL WITH HIM!'

Still cursing and screaming, the charging phantom closed the last few yards. *'Maybe this'll teach thee to inter-fere . . .'*

With his stick still high above his head he moved towards the priest. But as he saw Father Boniface's resolute expression and the steely blue eyes, he hesitated. He raised the stick higher still and took another step forward, *'Let this be a lesson to thee . . .'*

The priest fumbled under his coat around his neck and pulled out a gold cross and chain. As soon as the phantom saw it, he staggered backwards. The priest handed it to Billy. 'Hold it out towards him!'

Billy took the cross, held it out in his outstretched palm and walked towards Eli Knapp. The hideous spectre fell to the ground and floundered on his back. Father Boniface walked up to Billy's side and raised the shotgun.

'*Thou shalt not kill!*' the sprawling phantom screamed at him. '*Tha'r a man o' God! Tha can't slay me! In any case . . . ah'm dead already!*'

Billy looked down at the pathetic figure as it spat and cursed and slithered like a reptile back along the ground.

It was true what the teachers at school had always told them – *all bullies are cowards deep down* – and this bully was more cowardly and slimy than all the others put together.

Billy walked up and loomed over him. 'It's not us you have to worry about. We'll just wait until your stepson gets back . . . let him have his revenge.'

The phantom raised himself up onto his elbows and stopped cursing. He drooled and whined like an injured animal, staring over Billy's shoulder – his eyes filled with terror.

And then Billy froze as he sensed what the evil spectre was gawping at . . .

Goosebumps spread across his body. He'd stupidly allowed the hideous figure to distract him.

It was too late!

He could feel the icy stare . . . smell the animal scent.

The Moonwailer was crouched right behind him . . . *close enough to reach out and touch!*

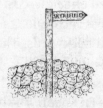

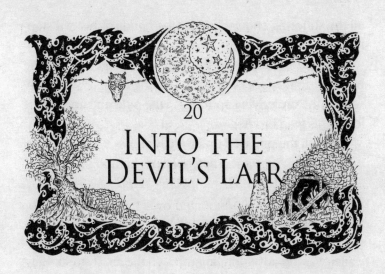

20
INTO THE
DEVIL'S LAIR

'*SHOOT IT, DAMN THEE!*' the cringing figure screamed.

Billy swung round and found himself staring straight into the eyes of the Moonwailer. It crouched only metres away, hissing and snarling.

For the first time he saw the Moonwailer's head in hideous detail.

The face was rounded, like a human head, but covered in sprouting hair. The ears were pointed . . . tipped with tufts of fur. The mouth dog-like . . . lips curled back . . . fangs drooling with saliva.

'D . . . d . . . don't move!' Father Boniface stammered. 'Just stay still!'

As the creature took a step nearer, Billy saw the pale yellow eyes staring straight at him. They were truly terrifying eyes, filled with hate, tormented and revengeful for all the suffering endured under the hands of his evil step-father . . . *Eli Knapp!*

. . . And then he saw through the savage face of the beast . . . to the face of a boy . . . young Isaac . . . and Billy sensed the underlying sorrow . . . the pain and anguish of losing his twin brother.

Billy felt the pity well up inside him.

A pathetic voice screamed out from behind:

'SHOOT THE BEAST . . . DAMN THEE . . . 'AFORE IT TEARS US ALL TO PIECES!'

Father Boniface lowered his gun and stepped to one side. Billy and Calum followed his example, but the Moon-wailer was already springing through the air. It struck Billy on the shoulder and sent him reeling sideways.

The cringing form of Eli Knapp screamed as the Moon-wailer landed on his prostrate body and sank its fangs into his throat. At the same time it tore at his flesh with claw-like hands.

'MERCY! MERCY!' the wretched man shrieked.

'QUICK! FOLLOW ME!' Father Boniface yelled at the two boys.

Without looking back, the priest and the two boys ran on past the Devil's Tooth and down along the same path that Quicksilver had sprinted for his life.

On, on they ran . . . Father Boniface in front, Billy following and Calum at the rear. The path became darker. The sides of the hills closed in. The ground became treacherous . . . littered with boulders.

And then they reached the log fence. Billy recognised it immediately as the 'gateway' to Howling Ghyll.

Father Boniface gasped and panted. 'OK . . . stop for a minute.' His face was a deathly white colour. 'We . . . we've done what we had to do. I'm not sure quite how . . . BUT WE DID IT!' God was truly on our side tonight. Two spirits have been reunited and justice done. They should now be released from their earthly existence and sent back to where they rightfully belong.'

Calum nodded. 'I can guess where Eli Knapp will finish up . . . down in the depths of hell?'

'Exactly!' the priest nodded, still trying to get his breath back.

'And the Moonwailer?' Billy asked nervously, handing back the priest's cross and chain.

Father Boniface took it and put a reassuring arm around his shoulder. 'We should pray that he is free from the devil and at peace . . . poor wretch!'

Billy frowned . . . went quiet . . . looked very thoughtful.

Calum and Father Boniface stared at him . . . as if he knew something. *And Billy did know something.* His sixth sense was growing stronger all the while.

He stood quite still, facing back up the deep ravine, sniffing the air and straining his ears. Apart from a nearby hoot of an owl, everything had gone deathly quiet.

'He's still with us,' Billy said in a quiet whisper.

'Please, no!' Calum exclaimed. 'What makes you think that?'

Billy hesitated, then concentrated again. 'Eli Knapp is gone. But while ever his brother's grave is still there, he'll be around to guard it. That was part of his deal with the devil. And right now he sees us as a threat. He's after us!'

The priest tensed. He tightened his grip on the gun and beckoned Billy and Calum to climb over the fence.

'Then we have no choice . . . we have to face him again. But not here! We have to get to the other end of the ghyll

. . . to where the beck springs from the ground.'

Calum almost shoved Billy out of the way to climb over the fence. Never had Billy seen his friend so scared. To make matters worse, another heart-stopping howl sounded from the head of the ravine.

Billy was right . . . the beast was still at large . . . and it had their scent.

. . . And their only line of retreat was through the creature's lair – the deep dark hollow of Howling Ghyll.

As Calum sprinted off into the darkness, Billy followed close on his heels. The priest, clutching onto his shotgun, trailed at the back.

*

Twice Calum fell over. The first time he slipped on a boulder and grazed his right knee. The second time he tripped over a twisted tree root and cut his left ankle – it really hurt, but at least it wasn't broken. Billy caught his face on a sharp branch clawing out from of one of the twisted trees and a trickle of blood ran down his cheek. The priest seemed in a state of panic. He struggled to keep up with them, moving more slowly, periodically turning and aiming his shotgun into the darkness.

Another blood-curdling howl told them that the boy-beast was much closer than before. Billy sensed the rapid ground it was making on them.

'WE'VE GOT TO GET TO THE WATER!' the priest yelled to the two boys. 'WE'RE ALMOST THERE!'

The desperation in the priest's voice spurred Calum on at the front. With his torch illuminating the litter of boulders, he and Billy hopped from one to another, desperate to hear the sound of running water.

The priest stumbled on, constantly looking behind. Three times he fell forward and almost smashed his face on the rocks. The gun twice fell to the ground. 'YOU CARRY ON! GET TO THE WATER!' he shouted ahead. 'I'LL HAVE TO STAY HERE AND FACE THE BEAST!'

But instead Billy stopped and went back to him. Calum did the same.

They found Father Boniface sitting on a rock. He looked ashen and exhausted.

'We're almost there, Father! I can hear the sound of running water . . . just round the next bend,' Calum said.

Father Boniface took a firm hold on the gun. 'You two go on . . . I'll join you later. I need to finish this here and now.'

Billy knew exactly what the priest meant. 'You're going to shoot the Moonwailer!'

Father Boniface nodded. 'I'm going to try! I thought after getting his revenge on his evil stepfather, he might have gone . . . but I was wrong.'

'I know. It's like I said . . . he's still guarding his brother's grave,' Billy sighed.

The priest nodded. 'The bond between those twins was stronger than we can ever know.'

Billy's heart skipped a beat as a shadow moved somewhere to his left, halfway up the steep limestone slope. He glimpsed it out of the corner of his eye.

'Don't move . . . it's here!'

'Wh . . . where?' Calum asked, his voice beginning to tremble.

'Up there . . . to our left. He's watching us.'

The priest turned slowly . . . aimed his gun up the dark craggy slope. 'Point your torch up there, Calum,' he whispered. 'Don't be afraid!'

Calum scanned the limestone cliff with the powerful beam. As the torchlight fell on a twisted tree high up on the slope, there was a rustling sound.

'He's . . . he's under that tree,' Calum stammered.

They all watched as Calum concentrated the torch beam on the tangle of branches. '*There!*' Calum gasped.

Sure enough, like cat's eyes, the eyes of the Moonwailer stood out in the strong light. The beast was crouched behind the tree . . . watching them.

'So what do we do now?' Calum asked, his voice quaking.

'Just stay calm,' Billy said, 'and pass me that plastic wallet . . . the one in your rucksack.'

'But . . .'

'*Just do it!*' Billy said firmly.

Father Boniface said nothing. He was completely entranced by the piercing eyes staring down at him. He supported the barrel of the gun on his metal arm and fingered the trigger with his good hand . . . aiming it straight towards the tree.

Calum kept the torch trained on the beast and at the same time eased his rucksack off his shoulder. He rifled in one of the pockets for the wallet. 'Here!' he uttered, passing it to Billy. 'But I still don't know what you want it for?'

There was more movement above.

Father Boniface yelled out, '*He's going to spring . . . get behind me!*'

But it was too late. The beast had already leapt out from the shadows and was bounding down the slope. The priest fired his first shot.

'BANG!'

Billy saw the spurt of blood as the silver bullet took away the tip of the beast's left ear.

But it just kept on coming.

Only metres away . . . BANG! The second silver bullet struck the Moonwailer's left knee. A small shower of blood and bone fragments sprayed out in the wake of its charge.

But it just kept on coming.

The shocked priest didn't get a chance to fire again – the gun needed reloading. The beast descended onto his prey. Father Boniface cried out in pain as the Moonwailer clawed at his neck.

Calum jumped back, picked up a heavy rock and hurled it at the attacker. It struck the Moonwailer on the side of the head and sent it sprawling across the dried up riverbed.

But the beast was quickly back on its feet and ready to spring again. It glared at Calum, spat at Billy and looked back at the helpless priest.

'IT'S ME YOU WANT!' Billy screamed at the creature. 'I WAS SENT HERE TO GET RID OF YOU . . . AND YOUR BROTHER!'

The last three words caused an instant reaction. Its face contorted, twisting into an expression of total ferocity . . . its attention now focused solely on Billy.

Billy fumbled in the plastic wallet, slid out the small rectangular mirror and clutched it in his right hand. The Moonwailer crept towards him.

Father Boniface wrestled with the gun, tried to right himself and reload it.

Calum picked up another rock and lifted his arm.

'No!' Billy said calmly. 'Stay still!'

Calum dropped his arm by his side.

Billy took a deep breath and swallowed hard. The Moonwailer hissed and snarled, fangs bared; claw-like hands at the ready . . . totally unaware of its torn ear and shattered knee.

It screamed and sprang.

Billy was knocked flat onto his back. The creature sat astride his chest, lowered its head and bared its fangs towards his neck. Quick as a flash Billy brought up the small rectangular mirror and thrust it into the horrific face.

The glass cracked across the beast's nose. It screamed in frustration and reared its head for a second strike.

Billy held onto the mirror, clasping it under his attacker's face. As the fangs came down a second time, the Moonwailer caught sight of its reflection.

It stopped . . . froze . . . staring at its dual image in the cracked glass. The face began to change . . . all signs of aggression evaporating. The eyes welled-up with sadness . . . the expression turned to one of anguish.

Billy wriggled free and edged backwards on his elbows.

The Moonwailer scrambled back to its feet and stood erect. It turned towards the head of the ghyll and stared up at the crescent moon . . . standing out brilliantly in the last hours of darkness.

It straightened its spine . . . raised its arms . . . and let out a fearsome howl of defiance. 'HHHOOOOWWWW-WOOOOOOOOO . . .'

'BANG!'

The priest's third shot struck its target.

The 'silver spear' pierced the beast's heart. The Moonwailer fell forward onto the ground . . . and moved no more.

Billy sat up and burst into tears. He wasn't sure why. Relief? Shock? Or was it because he felt truly sorry for the miner's boy who had been so maltreated and had been forced to endure so much?

Calum ran over and gawped down at the prostrate body as Father Boniface rolled it over onto its back.

'BILLY! COME HERE . . . QUICK!' Calum called to him.

Billy dragged himself to his feet and sauntered over to his friend. He looked over Calum's shoulder and saw the cause of his reaction.

The body of the Moonwailer beast had changed.

No more the ferocious animal that had terrorised the surrounding hills for so long – now just the naked slender body of a young boy. The eyes were open . . . staring blankly upwards . . . not piercing or accusing any more. The expression on the dead face was a mixture of curiosity and bewilderment.

Father Boniface closed the lifeless eyes and uttered a prayer. He felt in his pocket for his cross and chain and hung it around the dead boy's neck. 'I have one last job to do,' he said. 'In the meantime, I want you two to go straight back to the campsite. The police and heaven-knows-who-else will be waiting. Say nothing of this. Tell Elvis and his father to stick to the "wild dog" story. All will be forgotten in the weeks ahead . . . believe me.'

Billy and Calum nodded solemnly, Billy still wiping the tears from his dirty, bloodied face. They left the priest to his business and headed to the end of the ghyll towards the reassuring sound of running water.

When they finally reached the underground spring, the source of Howling Beck, they found Quicksilver lying injured on the far side of the stream.

The dog yelped in pain and wagged his tail at the same time.

'*He's still alive!*' Calum shrieked. He examined Quick-silver's badly bitten front leg and patted his head affectionately. 'He must have got attacked just before he reached the stream. It's lucky he managed to struggle the last few yards.'

The dog panted enthusiastically, but couldn't get up.

'What is it about water, Billy? And why the mirror?'

'It's like Father Boniface said . . . water *is* a mirror!' Billy replied. 'It reflects the truth. Would you want to see your reflection if you'd turned into a beast?'

'Suppose not!' Calum said. 'Seeing his reflection must have shocked him rigid. That's clever, Billy!'

The two friends tried to coax Quicksilver to his feet, but the dog lay exhausted, still in a state of shock.

'One of us will have to stay . . . you go and get help,' Billy ordered.

'OK, but we'll need to stick to the same story,' Calum said.

'What shall we say?'

'Well . . . we sneaked out of the tent to have a look round . . .'

'Duder will do his nut!'

'I know . . . we can't help that. We sneaked out . . . came across Elvis and his dad. Phoned for an ambulance. The dog went missing . . . and we went on to look for him!'

Billy looked down at Quicksilver. He was licking his injured leg. 'And we found him,' Billy said smiling. 'But who phoned for the ambulance?'

Calum rifled through his rucksack and brought out a mobile. 'I did!'

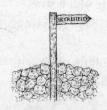

21
RETURN
JOURNEY

Back at the campsite things went more smoothly than Calum could have hoped for. There was no sign of any emergency services, no police, not even any lights – the tents were in darkness.

But as Calum climbed over the fence, crossed the beck and entered the campsite, a voice called out to him.

'Hey . . . what do you think you're up to?'

Calum had no choice but to go over to the figure standing by the entrance. It was the farmer, David Jessop.

'I couldn't sleep,' Calum said sheepishly.

'I'm not surprised!' the farmer said. 'I suppose you heard the helicopter. It's a wonder the whole campsite isn't awake.'

'That's what woke me,' Calum said using his wits. 'What was it? Has something happened?'

The farmer nodded. 'Two of those travellers . . . a young lad and his father . . . out snaring rabbits, by all account. The man got hurt. Not sure yet what happened. It'll all be in the local paper before long.'

'What about the boy?' Calum asked, desperately trying to think what to say next.

'Is he with his dad?'

'No doubt! They were both taken off in the whirlybird.'

The farmer asked Calum why he was fully dressed and just as Calum replied that he and his friends never bothered with pyjamas, a police car cruised up to the entrance.

Calum's heart began to race as the window of the police car slid down. 'Hi, David. Everything alright?'

'Yes . . . this young lad was woken up with the helicopter.'

The policeman looked Calum up and down. 'Do you always sleep with your clothes on?'

The farmer laughed. 'Seems so! That's young lads for you! Have you heard anything from the hospital?'

The policeman nodded. 'I've just come from there. We've taken statements. Seems the man was attacked by a wild dog. It's got to be the same one we're after. I think we're going to have to close the footpaths until it's caught.'

'That's a beggar!' the farmer moaned. 'Less footpaths . . . less walkers . . . less campers!'

'Sorry, pal . . . needs must!'

The window closed and the policeman drove away. The farmer turned back again. He looked anxious. Calum wondered if the farmer knew the real cause of the problem.

'You don't happen to have a first aid kit handy do you?' Calum asked. He reached down to his ankle where he'd cut it earlier. The wound was covered in dried blood.

'Have you caught your leg on something, lad?'

'I think so!' Calum replied innocently.

The farmer reached into the rear of his four-wheel drive. 'Here . . . take this . . . you can give it back in the morning.'

More good luck, Calum thought to himself. 'Thanks . . . goodnight!'

'Take care, lad. Don't let your teacher find you out of your tent!'

Calum returned straight to his tent, but only to get a sleeping bag. And then he went straight back to Billy. Between them they managed to bandage Quicksilver's injured leg and using the sleeping bag as a stretcher, carried him back to the campsite. They smuggled the dog into their tent and the three of them fell exhausted into a deep sleep.

*

The next morning the three weary adventurers awoke to the sound of the tent flaps opening. It was Elvis.

His freckled face beamed when he saw his beloved dog resting there with his new-found friends. '*Wow! Fantastic!*' was all Elvis could say.

They sat and exchanged stories and Calum asked Elvis to stick to the 'wild dog' story.

'May as well, anyway!' Elvis said, shrugging his shoulders. 'Dad went on and on about the beast boy and all that, but none of the doctors or nurses would believe him. They just thought he was del . . . deli . . . dilee. . .'

'Delirious!' Calum finished for him.

Half an hour later Elvis had taken Quicksilver back to the caravan camp 'to get him sorted properly', as he'd said, and Billy and Calum were eating cereals and bacon butties with the rest of the Year 7s.

'I can't believe we got away with it,' Calum said. 'Did it really happen . . . all that, last night?'

'I know. It was more like a dream,' Billy spluttered over a mouthful of cereal.

'More like a nightmare!'

'Come on you two . . . you look half asleep!' Matthew said to them in his usual bouncy way. 'We're having a sports day today. I hope you're up for it!'

'They'd better be up for it!' Sam called over to them. 'Some of us are going to take the girls on at netball . . . we can't afford to let them win!'

'You've no chance!' Kelsey snapped back at him. 'Anyway . . . there are only three of us . . .'

'And me!' Miss Dingle smiled, parading in a trendy tracksuit and designer trainers. 'Don't forget me!'

'I'll make your team up,' Oliver said solemnly. 'I'm very familiar with the rules of netball. My grandmother was a champion.'

The other Year 7s laughed. 'There's an offer you can't refuse!' Calum said cheekily.

Billy took another bite of his bacon butty and looked up at the sky. The crescent moon had long gone. Now the sky was blue, with white fluffy clouds and the sun was shining. At last it was more like summer!

Calum passed him the ketchup – it came out with a loud spurt.

'Brilliant!' Billy thought to himself. 'Absolutely brilliant!'

EPILOGUE

In the dead of night, a mysterious figure carried a young boy's body up through Howling Ghyll and on towards the Devil's Tooth. Reaching the mysterious stone, he dug a deep hole at its base and buried the boy's body alongside that of his twin brother. He carved the initials IK beside JK and added the words:

*May these two stray lambs be reunited
with their heavenly shepherd!*

His job done, he uttered a prayer, blessed the stone, and disappeared back into the brooding hills.

THE END

About the author: Peter J. Murray

 Pete has always been a story-teller and a practical joker. Twenty five years in teaching gave Pete the ideal opportunity to entertain his pupils with stories of spooky characters and unusual happenings, which led to the creation of many of the characters in his books.

Four years ago, Pete gave up his day job to become a full time author. He now visits over 150 schools a year, both in the UK and overseas, inspiring and enthusing children about reading, writing and being creative.

Pete self published his first book: Mokee Joe is Coming in 2003 and immediately won the prestigious Sheffield Children's Book Award, voted for by 112 schools. The rest, as they say, is history.

Peter lives with his wife on the edge of the Yorkshire Dales. He says that the hills and limestone scenery offer a constant source of relaxation and inspiration - in fact, they also provide the setting for this book!

www.peterjmurray.co.uk

Also by Peter J Murray

Mokee Joe Is Coming

The first book of the Mokee Joe trilogy.

What has poor Hudson done to bring upon himself the wrath of the evil shadowy figure of Mokee Joe? Thank goodness he has his friends Molly and Ash to help him . . . and, of course, the mysterious Guardian Angel.

Mokee Joe Recharged

The second book of the Mokee Joe trilogy.

Mokee Joe is back . . . stronger than ever, but Hudson is growing stronger too. The battle resumes as Hudson, Molly and Ash once more go through a series of terrifying encounters.

School life will never be the same again . . . and perhaps the idea of a spooky school disco was not such a good idea after all!

Mokee Joe The Doomsday Trail

The final book of the Mokee Joe trilogy.

There is a real twist in this final epic battle between good and evil as Hudson and his friends once more face up to the ultimate terminator.

We don't want to give away too many clues, but the setting for this book is incredible to say the least . . . suffice to say that you may never feel safe again after reading this gripping final instalment!

Bonebreaker

This is the first of the 'Bonebreaker' trilogy. Our new hero, eleven-year-old boy Billy Hardacre, finds himself involved in all sorts of spooky goings on at home. When he escapes on a holiday with his best friend, Calum Truelove and his family, things go from bad to worse. How could poor Billy ever have guessed that he is the descendant of an unfortunate Saxon boy, a victim of the ruthless Viking warrior known as the Bonebreaker? And now it's up to Billy to exact revenge.

Dawn Demons

Oh dear! Billy Hardacre seems to encounter strange happenings wherever he goes. A holiday at Aunt Emily's at the seaside surely must give him a well-earned rest. But as soon as Billy and Calum arrive in the vandalised sea-side town, they discover a terrible secret. A small army of deadly sailor dolls are in hiding. At dawn they emerge from a most unusual hiding place and wreak havoc and destruction on the town's inhabitants. Billy and Calum take it on themselves to do battle with the demons – but only with the aid of Bunty – a most unusual girl!